"THERE'S BE_____E COAST OF C_____ ____ ____ with kids."

Farnsworth fell in beside Sacrette. "Kids?"

"Kids." He replied flatly. "The skipper wants us to stand by for a briefing as soon as a special delegation from the UN comes aboard." He checked his watch.

Farnsworth opened the hatch for Sacrette. "In what mode do you want the birds readied? Strike? Or fighter?"

Sacrette's green eyes suddenly sparkled. A strange, challenging grin stretched across his mouth. "Fighter!"

Sacrette disappeared, saying nothing more. It wasn't necessary, thought Farnsworth, who recognized the look. He had seen it before. It was the look of a wolf smelling the blood of his prey.

Another hunt was on.

STRIKE FIGHTERS

TOM WILLARD

Harper Paperbacks

Harper & Row, Publishers, New York
Grand Rapids, Philadelphia, St. Louis, San Francisco
London, Singapore, Sydney, Tokyo, Toronto

This is a work of fiction. The characters, incidents, and dialogues are products of the author's imagination and are not to be construed as real. Any resemblance to actual events or persons, living or dead, is entirely coincidental.

Harper Paperbacks a division of Harper & Row, Publishers, Inc.
10 East 53rd Street, New York, N.Y. 10022

Cover illustration by Atilla Hejja

First printing: August, 1990

Printed in the United States of America

HARPER PAPERBACKS and colophon are trademarks of Harper & Row, Publishers, Inc.

This novel is dedicated to Brent Steven Willard, the last in a very, very long line; to the carrier-based fighter pilots of the United States Navy and Marine Corps: the best of the best. And to the toughest anti-terrorist hostage-rescue commandos on the face of the earth: the United States Navy SEALs!

STRIKE FIGHTERS

Prologue

1830.

THE WARM BREEZE OFF THE MEDITERRANEAN WAS from the south, carrying with it the smell of rain, which could be seen in the distance, falling in long, slanting gray columns from dark cumulus clouds moving slowly across Agios Nikolais, an ancient fishing village carved into the mountainous coastline of northern Crete.

In the bay, the outline of the *World Friendship*, a three-masted sailing schooner, jutted prominently from the pitching surface, naked of sail, except for a storm jib unfurled at the bowsprit, steadying the anchored vessel into the wind.

Teenagers roamed the wet, highly polished decks, wearing white T-shirts emblazoned with the symbol of the United Nations. Music drifted up from the main salon belowdeck, where others gathered, dancing, eating, talking in a variety of languages.

They ignored the weather. Sun. Rain. Nothing seemed to interfere with their spirits. Nothing seemed important except that they were together, sharing the adventure of a lifetime.

Ten miles offshore, the sun burned brightly; the sky was clear, blue, matching the Mediterranean at the horizon where distinction between sky and water was impossible.

A lone freighter plowed lazily along the surface. Her speed slowed to a crawl, indicating that the ship was either in trouble or bent on maintaining a position off the rugged coast.

Captain Giorgios Raspides stared through binoculars from the bridge of the *Helenas*, his thoughts wandering from the approaching weather to the danger on the well deck below, where nine fanatics lay stretched in obedient reverence.

"Mother of God," Raspides spit hatefully. "They are only children."

On the deck, nine Palestinian teenagers lay prostrate on the scorching metal deck.

Twenty feet away, two zodiac rubber boats sat filled to the oarlocks with rucksacks, AK-47s, and RPG-7 rocket launchers. Beyond the zodiacs, in the shadow of the forward mast, ten fifty-gallon containers, painted yellow, were stacked in a semicircle.

Raspides looked contemptuously at the tools of destruction, then again at the children who continued to remain silent in prayer. He shook his head, momentarily regretting having taken the money he had been paid for transporting the guerrilla force.

"Suckling babes should be at their mother's breasts. Not praying for God to help them commit murder," he said.

"They are Ashbal. Children of the Intifadeh," interrupted a harsh voice.

Raspides turned to Mohammad Jemal, a tall, sapling-lean Palestinian. His chapped lips curled with hostility, revealing teeth the color of porcelain beneath a drooping mustache. He wore a black shortsleeve wet-suit top; a jagged scar ran from his left elbow, disappearing into the folds of his armpit.

Raspides grumped disapprovingly. "Ashbal. Intifadeh. Call them what you like. They are children." Raspides pointed toward Agios Nikolais. "Like the children aboard that ship."

"Not like those children. Only a fool would fail to see the difference."

Raspides chuckled. "Fool? No, *fendi*. Not a fool. Just a sad old man who's seen too much change in the world. Too much violence."

Jemal pointed to the *Friendship*. "They know nothing of violence. They only know luxury."

Raspides nodded slowly. "Yes. Luxury. The luxury of childhood." He stared hard at the Palestinian. "And you will change all that. You and your nine lion cubs from the Libyan desert."

Jemal said nothing in response. His black-diamond eyes shifted to the well deck, to the single youth stretched out in front of his eight comrades.

Kahlil Salaman lay soaking in his sweat, his body facing Mecca, his thoughts on Allah, whose divine protection he had implored for nearly an hour. Pausing to glance over his shoulder, he carefully examined the faces of his soldiers, all boys, except Layla, the dark-eyed teenager from Nablos.

Layla was tall, slim, with long legs and budding breasts, which, on more than one occasion, had incited flames in the loins of her comrades. Unlike the boys, who were veterans of the *intifadeh*, "stone war" in Gaza, Layla had joined the commando team in the Libyan desert only four weeks earlier.

"They are *mujihadeen*," Jemal reminded Raspides, who didn't appear impressed.

"Yes, I know. *Mujihadeen*. Holy warriors." He spit on the deck.

"Each has been blessed by a mullah with the last rites of jihad. They are anointed."

Raspides hawked, spitting again on the deck. "You make it sound so romantic. Only you avoid the truth. They are the walking dead. Dead. Except for the final passing. Dead children guaranteed a place in paradise. Denied a life on earth."

Jemal leaned through the window, shouting below, "Kahlil."

Kahlil looked up to the bridge, shading his eyes from the sun. His features were sharp, bedouin, like his ancestors' for thousands of generations.

Jemal brought his hands together, as though in prayer.

Kahlil recognized the signal that had ended their daily prayer session for the past few months.

The boy stood, walking among the others, tapping each on the shoulder.

"Finish your prayers."

The faces of the other children turned to the young leader. Rashid. Awad. Mohammad. Ziad. Hassan. Meheisi. Mustapha. Layla. Children lost in the tempest of the Middle East.

He watched as they stood, stretching their legs; hardened muscles flexed systematically. He searched for fear in their faces. Instead, he found a collective radiation beaming from their eyes.

He saw they were unafraid.

Instinctively, his hand went to a stone hanging

around his neck from a leather lace. As he touched the stone taken from beneath an olive tree in the yard where his home once stood, bitter memories returned. Again he saw the Israeli soldiers planting the explosives in his home. He heard the explosion that turned his family into the street as beggars. The stone, and the memories, were all he had to remind him of his childhood. Except for the hatred burning in his heart.

It was all he needed.

Turning to the others, his voice spoke without waver. "Allah be praised. The great moment we've trained for has arrived."

Thrusting their arms into the air, the nine soldiers of Palestine shouted, *"Thawra hatda nasra!"*

Revolution until victory!

2345.

Beneath the main deck of the *World Friendship*, two sleeping bays were separated fore and aft by the main salon. Lying in her bunk in the forward section designated for the girls, Ilyannha Lavi tossed restlessly, her thoughts on the end of the journey.

Saying farewell would not be easy. Four weeks at sea had built many friendships among the children, all part of a UN-sanctioned sailing cruise designed to promote peace and understanding through exposure and interaction.

"Ilyannha? Are you asleep?" The face of Brigitte LeVeaux, a young French girl, hung over the side of the top bunk above Ilyannha.

Ilyannha rose to the edge of her bunk. She shook her head, sending a mane of long, dark curls spilling onto her shoulders. Her eyes were dark, framed by strong features. She was Sabra. A child born and bred in Israel.

"No," Ilyannha replied.

Brigitte whispered, her voice somewhat tinged with fright. "Did you hear something strange?"

Ilyannha pricked her ears to the night. There was the sound of the wind howling, the waves lashing against the *World Friendship*. Nothing else.

"It's your imagination...or the cadets walking around on deck."

Brigitte smiled. "The cadets are so handsome." She fluffed her blond hair. "Especially Dar Stenhjem...the Viking. So tall. Strong. He looks like a god."

Ilyannha giggled. "They all look like gods." The naval cadets assigned from eight countries to crew the sailing vessel for the UN were all unusually good-looking. "My favorite is the American."

"He's too arrogant."

Ilyannha laughed softly. "He's supposed to be arrogant. He's an American!"

Brigitte started to speak; a heavy thud rippled along the hull of the *World Friendship*. "Listen. There's that sound again."

Ilyannha went to the porthole. As she opened the small window, a spray of wind and water splashed her face. Thrusting her head through the hole, she saw the waves rolling methodically in from the sea. In the distance a red marker buoy skipped crazily on the surface.

Above her, out of her vision, she heard the soft patter of feet moving across the deck.

"It's nothing," she assured Brigitte. "The cadets must be changing the watch."

2348.

Dar Stenhjem was dying.

His mouth was twisted open. Blinded by a tornado of lights swirling through his brain, he felt the consciousness begin to drain from his mind.

Standing at the fantail where he boarded in silence, Jemal tightened his grip from behind, pressing his thumbs into the styloid processes beneath the cadet's ears, paralyzing the central nervous system while his viselike fingers dug into the throat, shutting off the trachea.

Suddenly—a *crack!*

Stenhjem went limp as his trachea shattered. A rush of blood and air filled his senses, along with nausea, a signal that soon the pain would end.

Jemal felt him shudder, then fall limp. "You shall serve me in paradise," said the assassin, discarding the body onto the deck while turning to the nine shadows materializing along the railing of the *Friendship*.

Jemal flashed a hand signal. Three shadows darted for the bow where two unsuspecting cadets sat chatting near the foremast.

Kneeling in the darkness beneath the starboard rigging, Kahlil raised a pistol, sighting on the cadet's white jumper. His mouth went dry; his finger trembled, closing around the trigger.

The automatic jumped in his young hands. The 9mm bullet, muffled by the silencer threaded to the muzzle, cut through the base of the cadet's skull.

His first kill baptized him into the blood fraternity of the fedayeen!

The second cadet started to shout when—with

lightning speed—Kahlil fired once, then twice, hitting the young sailor in the throat.

The cadet lurched backward, careening off the foremast before pitching into Kahlil.

The young Palestinian smelled the cadet's blood, his breath. Staring into the eyes of the dying lad, Kahlil stepped back. Slowly the sailor slid to the deck, his white Annapolis jumper turning red from the blood-dark holes in his chest.

Throughout the *Friendship*, the night came alive with the muted sounds of the Palestinian death mechanism.

In his cabin, the captain barely rose from his pillow as a wire tightened around his throat. His last vision was the eyes burning through a slit in the balaclava commando hood worn by his killer.

His last thought centered on the youthfulness of the eyes. Eyes radiating with such hatred.

Awad let the body fall to the pillow, then calmly unwound the bloody wire.

In the crew's quarters, six unsuspecting cadets died in their sleep, ravaged by MAC-10 machine pistols.

Three minutes after the carnage began, an eerie silence drifted across the main deck of the *Friendship*.

Moments later, the silence was broken by the shouts of prodding voices. Screams of frightened children began to fill the deck.

A string of teenage children were led along the deck. Dressed in nightgowns, pajamas, some in shorts and T-shirts, the children who had sailed beneath the protective banner of the United Nations were hauled sleepy-eyed, bewildered, and frightened from their bunks.

"We have counted twenty-four," Kahlil reported.

Jemal appeared pleased. "Good. Prepare to set sail."

Turning to the storm beyond the bay, Kahlil's eyes filled with uncertainty.

Jemal squeezed the boy's arm. His voice was ice-cold. "Hoist the anchor. We must hurry."

Kahlil nodded, then darted toward the bow as a demanding shout pierced the air.

"What is the meaning of this!" From the end of the human string, a tall woman was trying to pull herself free from one of the Ashbal.

Jemal motioned to Rashid, a heavyset Palestinian, who was struggling with the woman.

Rashid shoved the woman forward, her arms flailing.

A suspicious look clouded Jemal's face. "Who are you?" he asked the woman.

"Elaine Winters." Her accent was American; her voice steady.

Jemal nodded slowly, as though suddenly remembering something important. "Yes. You are one of the chaperones assigned to the children."

Elaine wiped nonchalantly at a strand of blond hair clinging to the perspiration coating her forehead. "There are three of us."

"Where are the other two?" Jemal snapped.

Elaine shrugged. "In Agios Nikolais. One became ill and needed medical attention. Due to the storm, they decided to stay ashore. They are husband and wife."

Jemal's cold eyes scanned the line of children. A thought suddenly struck him.

Motioning for Layla, Jemal whispered in her ear. "There is one missing. Search the ship."

Layla hurried toward the waist hatchway, her AK-47 poised at the ready.

Moments later, Layla entered the main salon. The salon was hot, muggy from the humidity of the storm.

Carefully, she began searching the rooms joining the salon.

In the boys' bay she found nothing. Racing back into the salon, she paused at the door leading to the girls' bay.

She sensed movement beyond the door.

Raising her AK to the ready, Layla slowly turned the brass handle of the door.

Standing at the porthole, Ilyannha saw the light bleed through the crack at the door.

Hurry! she demanded of herself.

Quickly she released her passport, allowing it to fall among the other children's passports resting in the bottom of a pillowcase she held. She took a large seashell from a dresser and added it to the pillowcase for weight, following the instructions given them regarding an attempted hijacking.

Her arm was moving through the porthole when the sharp voice of Layla ordered, "*Stop!*"

Ilyannha glanced over her shoulder. The young Palestinian stood framed in the pale light, her weapon weaving menacingly from her hip.

With nothing for a weapon except her courage and defiance, Ilyannha released the pillowcase.

She heard a splash; from the corner of her eye, Layla could be seen charging forward.

The butt of the AK-47 crashed against her skull, sending Ilyannha sprawling to the deck.

A loud ringing erupted in her ears; she saw the

muzzle of the weapon inch toward her face. Knowing this might be her last moment on earth, the proud Sabra used her only remaining weapon.

She smiled, knowing the nationalities of the children would be protected from the terrorists—especially the two other Israelis in the group.

Then she was swallowed by a deep veil of darkness.

DAY
ONE

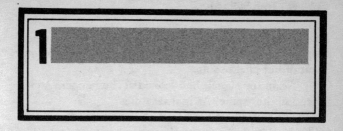

Arava Kibbutz. Negev Desert. Israel.

ZENA NESHER DROVE HER FINGERS DEEP INTO THE freshly tilled soil; her dark, sun-browned hands pushed the dirt carefully, sculpturing a small mound around the base of a tomato plant. When satisfied, she poured water onto the plant, spread the fragile branches apart, then scooped another hole in the long trough dug into the loam-colored garden behind her small house.

Zena was Sabra but didn't look Israeli. Her green eyes, framed within a shock of bright red, shoulder-length hair, suggested she was Irish or Polish—anything but Israeli.

Her fragile facial features, muscular legs, and superb physique suggested she was a model, or a dancer. Anything but what she was.

Which was a lawyer. And a soldier.

She paused only once, looking up to the shouts of children playing soccer near the concertina wire separating the security fence from the mine field surrounding the kibbutz.

Sasha, her nine-year-old daughter, squealed excitedly after scoring a goal. Zena smiled. The girls' team was giving the boys' team a shellacking.

As she reached for another plant, her outstretched

hand was suddenly frozen in midair by the sharp, gnawing signal from a communications beeper worn on the belt of her khaki shorts.

Again the signal. She looked at the beeper. A chill raced up her spine. As it always did.

She dusted off her hands and went into the house. The marble floors felt cool against her bare feet. The darkness of the room soothed the soreness of her eyes brought on by the hot, burning desert sun.

She went to her desk, quickly dialed a telephone number from memory, and waited for the answer. Seconds later, a familiar voice answered from Tel Aviv.

"Zena. Shalom!" The voice of Ehud Parizek was soft, pleasant, not the usual gruff, direct tone generally attributed to the director of the contracts department of the firm where she was employed.

"Ehud. Shalom." She waited. Ehud was not the type of man to make social calls.

"Zena, we have a contract dispute that requires your immediate attention." He used the word dispute carefully. He usually spoke carefully.

Zena tensed. If her instincts were correct, he would begin speaking cryptically. Ehud always spoke cryptically whenever a crisis involving contract matters had arisen.

Zena began writing on a notepad. "Who are the principals?"

"There are several. On the other side of the table, we are dealing primarily with a new company. One of undetermined nationality."

"What company will we represent?"

"Several, including one of Israeli nationality. An American company, and a number of foreign countries, mostly European."

"What are their terms?" She was asking for particulars, especially the type of hostages involved.

"Terms are unclear at present. However, the matter involves several minor questions requiring your expertise."

Zena checked her watch. "Can you send a helicopter?"

Ehud was quick with his response. "A helicopter has been dispatched. It should arrive within the hour."

"Will the negotiations be conducted in Tel Aviv?"

There was a long pause. Finally, Ehud answered. "No. One of our clients has arranged for the parties to meet aboard a yacht off the coast of Crete. You will be flown there this afternoon."

"Has the matter remained confidential?"

"Yes. Only the parties involved are privy to the negotiations. All communications will be kept 'in house.'"

Zena understood.

She hung up, then began deciphering the message from Ehud.

Situation. *Hostages.*

Principals. New company. *Terrorists nationality unknown.*

Company representing. *Other nations involved.* American. European.

Terms. *Unknown.*

Minor questions. *Children!*

Meeting. Yacht. *At sea.*

Privileged communications. *Top Secret.*

In house. *United Nations.*

She quickly rearranged the ciphered code.

Children from several nations taken hostage aboard a ship at sea by unidentified international terrorists. Matter being handled as Top Secret. Media unaware. Coordinating body the United Nations.

She didn't have to wonder. At least one, or more, was an Israeli.

Zena quickly packed. Arrangements were made for Sasha to stay with a neighbor who long ago had learned not to ask questions. The people of the kibbutz knew of the special "law" practiced by Zena Nesher.

Thirty minutes later the roar of an approaching helicopter filled the dry air above the kibbutz. Zena started for the door.

Near her desk, she paused, as though forgetting something. She reached into a drawer, removing a black 9mm Beretta automatic pistol. She dropped the pistol into her purse and went outside.

Sasha walked with Zena to the helipad.

Stepping into the sleek Huey 1-B, Zena threw her daughter a kiss.

The loam dust swirled around the child as the helicopter lifted off; there were momentary tears in Sasha's eyes. The tears were soon replaced with a broad smile reflecting her pride.

Moments later the helicopter disappeared on the horizon, taking with it Zena Nesher, special hostage negotiator for the State of Israel.

2

0930.

BOULTON SACRETTE, COMMANDER OF THE AIR GROUP (CAG), sat lopsided in the cockpit of his Strike/Fighter F-18B Hornet, his head resting against the canopy.

He wanted to curse, but fearing the damage he was certain any movement might cause, he simply sat motionless. Agonizing.

Never had his volatile French-Canadian blood pumped with greater impunity. His bloodshot eyes seemed to be roasting from the special pain that generally accompanies a hangover. Taped above the canopy jettison handle, his Pocket Rocket emergency checklist was nothing more than a blur; except the word EJECT, which, at that moment, he dreaded worse than the fires of hell.

Riding his fighter into the ground was a more pleasing alternative to making a "loud exit" with his head throbbing at Mach two.

Hot thermals punished the undercarriage, sending jolts of lightning through his skull; and if matters couldn't be worse, he would soon begin a Zone Five afterburner photo run through the Bekaa Valley south of Beirut.

The morning after his shipboard birthday party was turning into a mean son of a bitch!

"Wake up, sleeping beauty. Time to rock 'n' roll." The voice of his Dash Two—his wingman—Lt. Darrel Blaisedale, call sign "Blade," crackled through Sacrette's helmet.

Sacrette sat up quickly. Pain streaked through his head. He never realized words could be so painful.

Sacrette, running name "Thunderbolt," glanced out the canopy. Blade was easing onto Thunderbolt's three o'clock position off the starboard wing.

"How 'bout some 'Guns 'n' Roses'?" Blade held up a Walkman tape recorder.

"Stow the heavy metal. My head hurts. The less noise . . . the better."

"What's the matter, pappy? Getting too old for the night life?" Blade chided.

"Not the night life. Just the mornings after."

"Sounds like aviation menopause."

"*How nice,*" was Sacrette's only reply.

"How what?"

"How nice! It sounds better than 'up your ass!'" Sacrette laughed for the first time since waking up on two hours sleep.

There was a long pause from Blademan. "Roger, on the 'how nice.'"

"You're learning, son."

Blade came back quick, asking, "Why are we on this mission?"

Sacrette had asked himself the same question since being hurried from his quarters at 0500, given a quick briefing, then ordered to Alert Five status: buckled in and ready to launch in five minutes. Alert Five began at 0530. The two Hornets launched at 0730.

"This is what we do for a living, son. Keeping the

skies safe for the free world," Sacrette replied facetiously.

Blade laughed, replying, " 'How nice.' "

Sacrette was forty-three, a hard, tough forty-three. But not as resilient as his younger days. There was a time when he could drink all night, launch from a carrier deck on zero sleep, and bounce with the best MiG fighters in the sky.

The younger days. Time had moved fast for Sacrette. That was the way he preferred it. His mind flashed back, the recollections stirred by what lay dead ahead.

In the distance, the blue water of the Mediterranean ended against the white, pristine beaches of Beirut. Sacrette shook his head in disgust. He remembered Beirut—the old Beirut. The Beirut that was the Pearl of the Mediterranean. That was before the war. The hotel Napoleon. The bazaar on Hammurabi. The dark-eyed women. Beautiful women enjoyed by a young naval cadet on his first Med cruise during his senior year at the Naval Academy.

Then his first shooting war. Viet Nam. Battle Group Yankee Station. The Red River Valley of North Viet Nam. The SAM missile that blew his F-4 Phantom out of the sky. He still carried a photo of the *Double Ugly Rhino* disintegrating around him during ejection. The photo, taken by an alert photo reconnaissance technician flying 2000 feet above his six, was taped on the heads-up display of his canopy.

The photo reminded him of the past—while cautioning him about the future.

"Christ," Sacrette mumbled. He watched the devastated capital of Lebanon pass under the nose of his Hornet "Double Nuts," the numerical designation assigned to the CAG.

At twelve o'clock, low gray puffs of smoke splotched the Bekaa Valley, where Moslem artillery fired relentlessly into the city. Sacrette was cruising at Angel's eighteen, yet even at 18,000 feet above Lebanon he could see the city was nothing more than a shell. Like the carcass of an animal attacked by vultures; the shell was there, but everything inside was destroyed.

"You bastards really know how to screw up paradise." There was sadness in his voice. As though it were a soothing balm, the wretchedness of Beirut suddenly made him forget his personal misery, bringing him back to why he was streaking through the clear blue sky above Lebanon.

"Dash Two . . . Follow on my six." Sacrette glanced at Blade. His wingman saluted. As he raised the nose of his Hornet, Blade's aileron rolled over the top of Sacrette's fighter.

Sacrette nodded approvingly. "Not bad."

Two hundred feet below Sacrette's tailpipes, Blade checked in. "Dash Two on your six, Thunderbolt. Time to shake 'n' bake."

"Munchy . . . Time to go to work. I got the stick," Sacrette called to his Radar Intercept Officer buckled into the rear tandem seat.

The RIO, Lt. Juan Mendiola, earned his call sign "Munchy" while in flight school. His instructor nailed him eating a Snickers bar while inverted at Angel's thirteen.

"Roger, Thunderbolt. Camera's locked and loaded. Let's take some pictures of the bad guys. And by the way, thanks for the 'real time.'"

"No problem, kid. You can fly me anytime."

The RIO, a tough chicano kid from East L.A., was the weapons system officer. One of the best Thunderbolt had seen, and he had seen all the best. Munchy had flown the Hornet, banking some real pilot-in-command time while Sacrette slept after a shaky Cat Shot from the carrier USS *Valiant*.

"Eyes on the screen, Munch. We're on R.S.V.P. Keep your eyes out for party crashers."

Thunderbolt took the HOTAS, the hands-on throttle and stick, integrating aircraft control and weapons systems, shoved the nose forward, then signaled Blade he was on the hunt with the fighter pilot's battle cry.

"Fangs out!" the CAG barked the attack battle cry of the navy fighter pilot.

The F-18 screamed earthward from the sky. In that split second Sacrette forgot the hangover that had kicked his ass since departing the deck of the nuclear carrier USS *Valiant*.

Sacrette was now registering in "high confidence," that special mental mode fighter jocks accelerate into when their war machines go "Fangs out," into the foray where death becomes a notion that's purely in the abstract.

He felt the adrenaline surge; then as he hit 7.4 g's in a bat-turn to come on line with the Bekaa, he felt his speed jeans tighten around his legs and stomach and wondered in passing whether his testacles were cupped in tight.

No pain from the speed jeans. *Nuts were cupped*, he thought. *Line up, the valley's dead ahead off your twelve. Camera's on. Click. Click. Now. You know what's coming. Punch the cooker!*

Sacrette shoved the throttles past military power into Zone Five. An enormous surge followed when the twin GE F-404-GE-400 engines ignited into the afterburner stage. Thirty-five thousand pounds of thrust was generated as raw fuel was pumped directly into the hot exhaust flame, pushing the Hornet in front of a carpet of bright red fire.

The g meter blinked six . . . seven . . . eight.

Airspeed indicated 800 knots . . . 950 . . . accelerating.

The sky above the Bekaa ruptured as the Hornet thundered overhead, leaving a white trail from the transonic vapor wafting from the fighter's wing roots.

The photo run was completed within seconds. Sacrette glanced over his shoulder. "Hang on, Munch. We're going topside!"

Sacrette pulled the HOTAS back, thrusting the needle-nose craft upward.

The altimeter blinked wildly on the digitized heads-up display (HUD). Thousands of feet of elevation clicked off in seconds as Sacrette pushed the Hornet into a "pure vertical afterburner climb."

It was then he heard what he felt was coming since beginning the run!

"Gomers!" Munchy's console came to life as three blips appeared on his APG-65 radar screen.

From the ground, heat-seeking Morker missiles, guided by laser-beam tracking, were in hot pursuit.

Buzzers began sounding; the blips closed ground as the Hornet shot through Angel's sixteen.

"Flares!" Sacrette ordered.

Munchy fired the chaff/flare dispenser button. From the dispensers forward of the main gear well, parachute flares fired, etching the blue sky above Beirut with a trail of glowing iridescent light.

Glancing back at the flares, Sacrette was momentarily reminded of a long string of wet pearls.

An orange fireball shook the sky. Aftershocks followed as one of the missiles struck a flare.

"Go to ECM!" Sacrette ordered.

Sacrette's RIO began electronic countermeasures, jamming the airways with a multitude of signals designed to interfere with the radar-tracking device used by the Moslems.

Munchy watched the radar scope breathlessly as one of the Morkers flew toward the Syrian-occupied sector of the Bekaa.

"How nice!" Sacrette said aloud, watching the Morker explode against a hill where the Syrian artillery was entrenched.

"Fangs out!" the voice of Blade roared. Sacrette turned back for a quick glance. Blade was making his run through the valley.

A loud, piercing buzzer filled Sacrette's cockpit.

"They've locked us up!" shouted the RIO.

One of the missiles had locked onto the Hornet's enormous afterburner signature.

"Range!" Sacrette called to Munchy.

"Five thousand . . . Four thousand . . ."

Over the top! Over the top! Sacrette's instincts took command. Without thinking about what had to be done, he shoved the nose over, placing the Hornet in a vertical afterburner dive.

"Get us out of here, Thunderbolt, or in three seconds we'll be ass deep in the kimchi." Munchy's voice was as rock-steady as Sacrette's hand.

Thunderbolt Sacrette pushed his F-18 to the edge of the envelope, cranking off six-g bat-turns, aileron rolls, hammerheads, scissor moves, the whole maneuvering package acquired over his nineteen years as a fighter pilot.

Nothing seemed to work.

"I can't shake this gomer," Sacrette called to Munchy.

The RIO tried to sit forward in the pit as Sacrette pulled the nose into another vertical maneuver. His speed jeans inflated, tightening around his legs as the blood flow to his lower extremities was shut down, eliminating blood pooling, which led to unconsciousness.

"Two thousand..." Munchy's g-strained voice echoed over the radio.

Sacrette's vision was reduced to tunnel vision. Barely able to move his head, he thought not of the aircraft disintegrating under the tremendous stress. The Hornet could take any configuration inside—or outside—the envelope. It was the human factor. The men who flew the war machines. There was the vulnerability.

Sacrette's face twisted into the gargoyle look brought on by the g's.

Drawing from that special reservoir of experience and professionalism, he forced a smile, then laughed, telling Munchy, "There's one move left. Hold on, Munch."

"I'm not going anywhere."

"Give me the word at one thousand."

"Roger." Three seconds later, Munchy shouted, "One thousand!"

Sacrette activated the rear fuselage speed brake; simultaneously he raised the nose, chopped the power, and hung a quick Immelman.

Munchy's voice rose six octaves as the speed jeans inflated; his eyes felt as though they were being pushed, as though they would explode from their sockets.

With all his strength, the RIO raised his head and peered through the canopy. His face, which moments earlier appeared horrific as the skin contorted from the high-g 180-degree turn, suddenly transmogrified.

He smiled as the Morker shot past, streaking toward Syria only a few feet from the canopy.

"Yeah!" shouted Munchy. "You did it, Thunder! You did it. Now get us the hell out of here."

Sacrette was sitting forward, holding the HOTAS loose in his hand. His head was swirling as his brain tried to catch up with the rest of his body. The mixture of booze in his bloodstream and the high g's had pushed him out of SA—situational awareness.

Slowly he raised his head. The taste of blood was in his mouth; his gums were bleeding from clenching his teeth during the last evasive maneuver.

"Thunder . . . Thunder!" Munchy was shouting from somewhere close. Sacrette looked out on the wing. He saw the RIO dancing around a sombrero lying near the wingtip.

"Get your ass back in here, Munch!" Sacrette's voice was no more than a whisper.

"What!" Munchy called from the pit. Instantly the RIO saw that Sacrette was flying the Strike/Fighter from dreamland.

"Wake up, Thunder!"

The cloudy haze began to lift; Sacrette felt the heaviness of nausea and fatigue float away.

Seconds later, Sacrette's head cleared, only to hear the piercing voice of Blade.

"I'm hit. I'm hit. Pressure dropping in the port engine."

Sacrette's SA returned with the speed of his fighter. Glancing around, he spotted Blade's fighter streaking toward the blue-green water of the Med.

As he spotted a plume of black smoke, Sacrette's gut tightened and he rolled onto Blade's tail section.

"Blade. I'm on your six. Visual indicates you've taken a hit."

"Where?" Blade's southern voice sounded shaken, like a man who wished he were somewhere else.

"Shut down your left engine. The missile didn't explode. But you're taking it with you . . . stuck up your tailpipe."

There was a strained silence, and just before Blade's left engine quit burning, Sacrette laughed as his new Dash Two capped off a rather *dinki dao* morning.

"How fucking nice!"

3

1115. Battle Group Zulu Station.

THE CAPTAIN'S CABIN WAS SITUATED JUST A FEW FEET from the bridge; this design had a specific intent: to provide the captain with private quarters near the nerve center of the ship.

The USS *Valiant* sailed under the command of Captain Elrod Lord, a tall, strikingly handsome man with square-rigged shoulders. His weathered face appeared chiseled from stone, framing laser-green eyes that never seemed to rest.

Lord sat at his desk; the walls of his cabin were covered with photographs, mostly of airplanes he'd flown since his first carrier assignment during the Korean conflict. He couldn't remember the thoughts of the young pilot smiling at him from the cockpit within one of the frames; he did remember the plane. *Anna Lee*, named after his wife.

The FJ-3D Fury was shot out from under him during a knife fight over the skies of Korea with a MiG-15.

Other photographs chronologically portrayed the career of Captain Lord: an F-8 Crusader launching from the carrier *Coral Sea* at Yankee Junction; a Blue Angels F-4 Phantom, which had been replaced by the F-18A Hornet.

A wall filled with "tits machines," as the pilots referred to a hot aircraft. And memories. And jokers.

One particular photograph caught his eye, evoking a laugh as it always did. A young ensign sat in the cockpit of a Phantom.

On the pilot's shoulder, wearing a white sailor's cap, perched a chimpanzee.

Ensign Boulton Sacrette had roared onto the deck of the *Nimitz* with a chimp in his lap, saluted the CAG, who was Lord, and joined VFA-84.

The next day Lord discovered his first gray hair. Over the years, he would hold Sacrette personally responsible for the premature change of his hair from strawberry red to storm-cloud gray.

Not that Lord didn't understand the need for his pilots to be a little crazy; he was once that way. Now, as captain, he shed the cloak of zaniness for the starched severity of leadership. He was the man at the core of the battle group. Personalities surrounding him varied, but his remained as it had since becoming captain. Stoic. Resolute. Alone.

A battle group captain was surrounded by thousands of fighting men, yet he stood alone.

That was another design.

He turned to a knock at his door. "Come in."

A young ensign entered. "Sir. You're wanted in the CIC. Message from the Pentagon."

Lord followed the ensign through the narrow passageway leading to the flag bridge.

"Captain on the bridge," barked a marine guard.

The Combat Information Center was located aft of the bridge. It was the nerve center where the captain stood to command the ship during battle. Banks of radar scopes filled one wall; a map of the Med filled another, depicting transponder squawks from other ships of the BG.

Lord picked up a red phone and pressed a button near the mouthpiece. His words would be scrambled, transmitted to the Pentagon, unscrambled, and heard clearly at the other end.

"Captain Lord."

Lord listened intently. When he spoke, it was to the point. "How many hostages, Admiral?"

The question was answered.

"What are my orders?"

Five minutes later Captain Lord hung up the phone. What he had heard from the Pentagon had not made him happy.

He started through the bridge, pausing to glance at the empty sea as the voice of the Air Boss boomed over the MC-5 intercom on the flight deck.

"Emergency pull forward!"

Lord's unhappiness intensified.

4

CHIEF PETTY OFFICER DESMOND "DIAMONDS" FARNS-worth stood crossarmed, his teeth clamped around the chewed remains of his last Cuban cigar. He was standing in the shadows of the island, the massive superstructure rising from the flight deck of CVN 85 USS *Valiant*.

Farnsworth was fifty-two, trim, and muscular; he kept mumbling to himself, "I'm getting too old for this shit!" But he knew he was not. He was merely worried.

Worry came with the territory for the crew chief of the *Valiant*'s a*V*iation *F*ighter *A*ttack wing—VFA-101 Fighting Hornets.

His jaw was working feverishly, pushing his black skin upward where the folds above his brow collided with the smooth, razor-shaved scalp of his head. This automatically transformed his face into what appeared to be that of a pissed-off bulldog.

Diamonds wasn't pissed. He was thinking about what was happening—or might happen—on the flight deck in a matter of seconds.

Miles from the carrier Blade was approaching CVN 85 behind the controls of his disabled Hornet.

Which made everyone's ass aboard the *Valiant* suck up tight.

Men in green shirts, blue shirts, shirts of all colors, began moving into position on the deck. The color-coded shirts designated specific duties of the men.

The most dreaded color, the red of the firefighters, always brought a gut-wrenching uneasiness. As did the presence of the heavy emergency equipment.

The air was further electrified by the groan of Tilly, the huge crane, whose diesel engine broke the morning air. That was followed by Big John, the massive forklift used to clear the deck of disabled aircraft. Both machines lined up side by side, waiting like two huge dinosaurs.

Medics appeared from the battle dressing station, the emergency operating room in flight deck control. The BDS served only one purpose: to save those who could be saved until further surgery could be provided.

"Come on, Blademan . . . put her in the trap." Diamonds glanced at the arresting cables designed to stop the aircraft when joined by the fighter's grappler tailhook.

He raised a pair of binoculars and sighted the tandem-seat Hornet at the ten-mile approach point. He spoke softly to himself, "Don't shoot for the number three wire, son. Catch the first one available."

Diamonds knew the pride of the fighter jocks. The number three arresting wire was always their target. It was the pilot's final test for a "well done" flight.

Instinctively, he knew Blade was shooting for number three.

As though his thoughts were being transmitted over the headphones connecting him to the UHF communications system monitoring Blade's radio, a familiar, settling voice began talking to Blade.

Sacrette was following in the trail behind the crippled Hornet, talking in a calm voice.

"Go to down and dirty on your call, Blade. This is

the homestretch . . . everything looking good. Maintain straight and level. Shoot for wire one. Bolting the deck will ruin your day."

"Roger, Thunderbolt. Bird farm dead ahead," Blade replied. The *Valiant*'s flight deck came into view.

Blade retraced the throttles, slowing his Hornet to 180 mph. With a quick glance he followed the emergency procedure outlined on his plastic Pocket Rocket Checklist.

He started to speak when the voice from the Air Ops officer interrupted. "Blade. This is Home Plate. Call the Ball. You've got Charlie for landing. Good luck, sir."

Sacrette's calm voice again pierced the momentary static between communications breaks. "Left rudder, Blademan. Easy left . . . Don't let her drift . . . Don't bury the hatchet with your nose . . . Watch your altitude . . . You only get one grab at the brass ring."

"Roger, Thunderbolt . . . Easy left rudder . . . Power coming back."

Farnsworth could see the aircraft's angle of attack decrease after Blade eased back on the throttle, bringing the Hornet onto a cleaner glideslope. He released a slow sigh.

Thunderbolt gave his final instructions, telling Blade, "Give me a bad-to-the-bone landing, Blademan."

With that final word of encouragement from Sacrette all communications with the fighter ceased. Blade would need all his concentration to land the Hornet in what all the personnel aboard the carrier knew was the most difficult task known to aviation: making an arrested landing aboard an aircraft carrier.

On the flight deck there was silence. Firefighters leaned nervously from behind the heavy walls at the island, waiting—hoping they wouldn't be needed.

The barricade, the net system designed to stop the aircraft should Blade's hook miss the arresting wires, was erected and waiting, its meshing glowing beneath the morning sun. The whirring sound of elevator three lowering the last of the topside aircraft to the sanctuary within the bowels of the *Valiant* was the final signal to the crew, telling them the fate of the Hornet was now placed in the hands of Blade.

Seconds later, with wings waggling, Blade crossed the threshold. The air stung with the sudden silence when the Hornet's only operational engine was cut as Blade flared for landing.

A shrill whistling was heard. Breathing aboard the *Valiant* all but ceased. Throughout the ship over 6000 pairs of eyes were glued to hundreds of television sets depicting the event over closed-circuit television. The entire complement of the *Valiant* was locked into the crisis. Each man knew that under the most ideal of circumstances a carrier landing was nothing more than a controlled crash landing.

To land disabled was a pilot's worse nightmare beside being adrift at sea in a raft.

Blade hit the trap with a *crunch!* as the landing gear slammed onto the runway. Smoke boiled from where the tires found purchase.

Normal carrier landings are procedurally followed by what can only be described as a necessary act most pilots would consider counterproductive to the task at hand.

Once the aircraft cuts its engines, flares, and crunch lands, the pilot immediately shoves the throttles to full military power, in essence starting another takeoff run. This is done in the event of a bolter, where the tailhook has failed to engage with an arresting wire. Failure to engage, combined with the aircraft's forward speed, will send the plane rolling off the deck.

Power is again cut once the pilot feels the five-g force of the landing slam him deep into his seat.

If all goes well, the g force is the most welcome feeling in the world. If not, the fighter is running at maximum power, preparing for takeoff in what is nothing more than a touch-and-go.

That's not the case with an aircraft operating on a single engine with a hot rocket shoved up its pipe.

"Shit!" Diamonds breathed heavily. Blade's tailhook missed the first of the five arresting wires.

Then the second.

"God dammit. Grab!" the chief ordered.

In the next instant, as though obeying, the aircraft's tailhook joined the disabled fighter to the ship. The needle-nosed craft lurched upward, appearing to shudder, then jerked and settled to a sudden halt.

"Am I bad-to-the-bone...or am I bad-to-the-bone!" Blade's voice purred over the headphones.

Farnsworth clapped his hands. "Hot damn. Hot-diggidy-damn!"

From every point on the carrier, the voices of over six thousand sailors suddenly erupted in a loud, quaking cheer.

On the flight deck a wave of sailors began to swarm toward the Hornet. Diamonds was pulled along in the wave.

With each step Farnsworth began to change. First he was elated; then he appeared sullen. Finally, as he reached the aircraft, where Blade's smiling face appeared, Farnsworth looked like a man who could chew and digest nails.

Among the cheers, his loud, penetrating voice

erupted, "Damn you, sir. What in the mother-lovin' hell have you done to my aircraft!" Instinctively, he was saluting the pilot while unfolding the port folding ladder.

The deck fell into an ominous silence. The young sailors knew there was nothing more contrary than a crew chief who considered his aircraft to be his personal property.

Blade smiled, removing his helmet like a victorious knight who has just won the hand of a fair maiden. He was young, handsome, and cocky. The way fighter pilots are supposed to be. And he was intuitive, which allowed him to recognize when Diamonds was truly angry. This wasn't one of those times. It was just Diamonds's way of saying thank you.

"Sorry, Chief." Blade shook his close-cropped blond head. "You boys can fix this baby in no time at all." He pointed a challenging finger at Diamonds. "Which means, Chief, I want to be operational by zero-seven-hundred. Understood?"

A menacing smile etched the bulldog's face. He patted Blade's shoulder. "Aye. Aye. Sir." Then Farnsworth nodded toward the engine. The fins of the Morker could be seen jutting from the exhaust. "In the meantime, I strongly suggest you and your RIO get your young asses out of this aircraft. If that rocket decides to wake up . . . you might not be here at zero-seven-hundred."

Blade's face went slack as the exhilaration suddenly vanished. "I heard that, Chief."

In his cockpit, Sacrette shoved the throttles past military power into Zone Five, lighting the afterburners as raw fuel was injected straight into the engine's hot exhaust.

What followed was sheer ecstasy for the crew on the flight deck.

An earsplitting roar boomed sixty feet above the flight deck. The technique, called "flattening the hat," evoked another spontaneous cheer from the sailors.

All eyes turned to the sky where Sacrette's Hornet shot toward the sun in a pure vertical afterburner climb. At Angel's eighteen he went over the top, lowered the nose, diving straight at the *Valiant*.

Moments later, his g-stressed voice cracked over the radio, "Would you ladies mind holding hands some other time. I'm low on fuel."

The deck crew rolled Blade's Hornet behind a portable scatter-shield where the Morker would be carefully removed, then dispatched overboard.

Three minutes after Blade's Strike/Fighter touched the carrier surface of CVN 85, Sacrette crunch-landed in the trap, nailing the number three wire dead-center solid, then taxied to elevator three.

As he shut off the engines, a sudden blast of heat swirled from the nozzles of the turbofans. The canopy opened. Sacrette stood, returned the salute of the approaching crew chief, and flashed a brilliant smile.

He was tall, taller than most jet jocks, and deadly, thought Farnsworth, who had first met Sacrette in Viet Nam in 1972. Sacrette had been shot down over North Viet Nam. Miraculously, he escaped his NVA captors two days later—a matter of hours before he would have been routed to an obscure residence at the Hanoi Hilton.

Looking up at Sacrette, Farnsworth could still remember that day, and that dazzling smile. *Some things never change*, he thought. *No matter how much everything else changes*.

Farnsworth was with SEAL Team One when his team crossed trails with Sacrette near the DMZ while on a recon mission. They were reunited after the war, after wounds suffered by Farnsworth in the evacuation of Saigon forced him from the SEALs. He cross-trained as a crew chief and had been with Sacrette and VFA-101 since 1976.

Sacrette removed his helmet. His face was leatherlooking. *Each line a battle scar*, thought Farnsworth. Sacrette started to speak when Munchy touched him on the shoulder.

"Skipper. The captain wants you on the horn."

Sacrette pressed the communication switch on the mike connecting his helmet to Lord's gravelly voice.

Moments later Sacrette's smiling features melted into a tight frown. He softly replied, "Aye. Aye. Skipper."

Farnsworth lowered the folding ladder. Sacrette started down. Diamonds could see there was something troubling Sacrette.

"Problem?" Diamonds asked cautiously.

Sacrette nodded. "There's been a hijacking off the coast of Crete. A ship filled with kids."

Farnsworth fell in beside Sacrette as the CAG walked toward the island. "Kids?"

"Kids," he replied flatly. "The skipper wants us to stand by for a briefing as soon as a special delegation from the UN comes aboard." He checked his watch. "Maybe I can grab a couple hours of sleep."

Farnsworth opened the hatch for Sacrette, asking, "In what mode do you want the birds readied? Strike? Or fighter?"

The F-18 was a Strike/Fighter, capable of carrying an arsenal of bombs on a "mud mover" bombing mission, or easily converted to fighter mode for interceptor missions.

From within the grayness spilling out from the island

entryway, Sacrette's green eyes suddenly sparkled. A strange, challenging grin stretched across his mouth. "Fighter!"

Sacrette disappeared, saying nothing more. It wasn't necessary, thought Farnsworth, who recognized the look. He had seen it before. It was the look of a wolf smelling the blood of his prey.

Another hunt was on.

5

SACRETTE DROPPED INTO HIS BUNK, RAGGED FROM the fatigue. Slowly he stretched each muscle; muscles that ached from the flight, the g-stress, and, oddly enough, the crunch landing.

A single light burned above the sink in his private quarters, which were no larger than a prison cell. Windowless. Gray. A lonely cubicle; a place to come to for the mechanical necessities such as sleep, showering, and solace.

He tried to sleep, but gnawed by too much fatigue, he could only lie there, staring at the ceiling where a *Playboy* pinup smiled down from above his bunk, her body full and alluring.

Glancing to the wall opposite the sink, his eyes traveled over three photographs depicting the life experiences that progressively shaped him into what he was: a fighter pilot.

A destroyer of men and their machines.

One photograph of his Montana childhood captured him at twelve, standing on a frozen river, holding a beaver caught in his trap line.

Another showed him kneeling proudly by his F-4

Phantom aboard the *Coral Sea*, with Martini, his pet monkey, perched on his shoulder.

The third was a MiG 19 disintegrating over the Red River Valley of North Viet Nam.

His first kill. That single, voluntary act cold-bloodedly carried out in order to survive. A kill he conducted, like others, without ever seeing the faces of the dead.

That was a haunting question for all fighter pilots: What did their dead look like?

He no longer hunted and trapped, as his ancestors, who moved into the United States from Canada at the turn of the century, had done.

Martini was gone, lost when his Phantom was consumed by a SAM missile.

The memory of the MiG 19 remained vivid, as though it had happened moments before. Like the Libyan and the Iranian.

Gradually, his eyes began to close. Drifting off, he felt himself in flight.

He was alone, soaring through the sky like an eagle. Just before the curtain of sleep closed around him, he saw, on the horizon, another eagle approach.

A thin smile crept across his lips; his eyes tightened beneath the brow. His finger began closing around the trigger, when—suddenly—a sharp, metallic voice shrieked over the MC-1 intercom, "Commander Sacrette. Report to the ready room! On the double!"

6

1530.

The ready room of the *Valiant* was plush com-
pared to most carrier briefing rooms, serving as a com-
bination tactical discussion center, general hangout area
for the pilots, and trophy room.

The floor was richly carpeted in blue; brown, con-
toured leather chairs sat in neat rows. The front wall of
the room was lined with banks of television screens
plugged into a variety of communication systems ranging
from cable television to surveillance satellites roaming
the sky above earth.

Walking through the entryway, the first-time ob-
server was greeted by the red silhouettes of fighter planes
painted on the wall.

Two were Soviet-made outlines bearing Libyan
flags; the kill date was stenciled in white.

Four were Phantom F-4 outlines, bearing Iranian
flags.

This was the kill gallery of the *Valiant*.

Entering the room, each pilot would fondly pat the
silhouettes, which, in time, would gradually fade in color,
requiring repainting. No problem. It was the contact that
mattered.

The ceremonious reminder of what VFA-101 did for

a living: the destruction of enemy aircraft.

A commotion from the rear interrupted everyone's thoughts.

All eyes turned to the CAG. Sacrette was grinning beneath his hat emblazoned with the gold letters TOP GUN.

Sacrette entered with the arrogant swagger of the fighter pilot, flashing his perennial grin. Looking at the men, he knew what they were thinking.

Especially the pilots.

He still wore his speed jeans. Each stride was followed by a loud *Zing* where the nylon fabric rubbed.

It was the pilot's way of announcing that he was ready—for anything.

Pausing, he touched each silhouette as he passed, giving special attention to a Libyan MiG 25 Foxbat and an Iranian Phantom.

Sacrette's kills. The Foxbat was splashed over the Gulf of Sidra. The Phantom over the Persian Gulf.

Lt. Cmdr. Anthony "Domino" Dominolli, the VFA 101 exec, was sitting in the fourth row. His eyes twinkled expectantly as he watched Sacrette stroll down the aisle, as though he knew what the CAG was thinking.

Sacrette appeared pleased and, feeling that confidence was high, nodded approvingly at the thirty pilots and RIOs waiting for the order to launch into a hostile zone.

Showing their respect, the pilots started to rise. Sacrette extended his hands palm-down, telling his men, "Gentlemen. You may remain seated."

A voice spoke good-naturedly, telling the CAG, "You can leave at any time, Sacrette."

Glancing at Commander Lowell Stennard, exec for the *Valiant* SH-60B Seahawk covert ops/torpedo attack helicopter squadron, Sacrette smiled while his hands flashed from his side, mimicking a gunfighter drawing and firing.

As if on cue, all the pilots of VFA-101 echoed in chorus to Stennard.

"How nice!"

A wave of laughter rolled through the room as Sacrette sat down beside Domino.

"Rough morning?" asked Domino. He was short, with a thick bull neck. His hands were soft-looking, well manicured, like those of most pilots.

Sacrette shook his head. He started to speak when, suddenly, he jerked upright at recognizing the stunning redhead sitting in the front row. She sat flanked by three others, all men.

Without pausing, Sacrette marched briskly down the aisle.

One of the pilots whispered, "Fangs out! Thunderbolt."

All eyes in the ready room followed Sacrette.

At the front row, he paused, flashing a devilish grin to Zena Nesher, then bowed gracefully.

"Hello, beautiful." He bent and brushed his lips lightly across her cheek.

"Shalom, Boulton," Zena replied softly. She had met Sacrette in 1988, when the CAG delivered the first F-18A to her husband, a squadron leader in the Israeli air force.

He returned six months later in the darkest hours of Zena's life, after her husband's Hornet disintegrated over Lebanon.

Looking around, Sacrette gestured to the other pilots. "You're creating quite a stir. These guys haven't seen a woman in three months. Especially a beautiful woman."

She smiled. "I can take care of myself."

Sacrette winked. "You sure can." He turned to the other pilots ogling the reunion. "To hell with superstition. Right?"

The men in the ready room applauded and cheered.

While it's generally considered bad luck for a woman to be present aboard a fighting ship, and female naval personnel are restricted absolutely from sea duty, the personnel in the room seemed to delight in Zena's presence.

The men sitting beside Zena simply stared in astonishment.

Zena casually introduced the three men to the group commander.

"Gentlemen, this is Commander Boulton Sacrette. I suspect he will play a key role in the current crisis."

Sacrette shook hands with Hans Friedrich, a short, paunchy West German. Friedrich, a former member of the West German intelligence agency BND, was internationally famous as the negotiator of the Mogadishu hijacking in 1978. Currently, he was the assistant to the Federal Republic's ambassador to the UN.

"Commander Sacrette and I met briefly last year."

Slight embarrassment registered on Sacrette's face. "My apologies, Herr Friedrich. I don't recall."

A frown stretched across the German's ruddy face. "Ramstein."

Sacrette nodded methodically. He didn't recall the meeting. He did recall the place. "Yes. The air show."

Friedrich glanced at the others, telling them, "Commander Sacrette provided a splendid demonstration of his aircraft's capabilities at the Ramstein air show. If memory serves me, you preceded the tragic flight of the Italians. Correct?" His eyes seemed to cloud at the memory.

"Correct." Sacrette remembered. The smell of burning fuel and burning flesh still haunted his dreams.

A hush fell over the ready room. Zena, noting the awkwardness, continued the introductions. She introduced Gunnar Josephson, a tall, gaunt Swede, and Hector Delbusto, a Spaniard. Josephson nodded politely; Delbusto stood, offering his hand.

Sacrette started to speak when a loud command brought the personnel to their feet.

"Ten-hut!" the captain's yeoman barked.

The men jerked instinctively to attention as Captain Lord entered. All eyes followed his graceful form as he marched, ramrod stiff, to the podium.

"Gentlemen. This is the situation." Captain Lord held a pointer to one of the television screens. A blue-green blur appeared. Lord nodded at a technician sitting at a nearby computer console.

The technician punched in the number 150, the center of the electronic color spectrum that digitized the wavelength coloration that began with black at one end of the spectrum, to white at the opposing end. He pressed another computer key that photographed the area, then sat back, waiting for the image to project onto the screen.

When the picture clarified, Lord pointed at the sleek image in the center of the field. The imaging radar and cloud-penetrating satellite *LaCrosse* was transmitting from eighty miles above the Med since being moved on station by Houston NASA.

The white sails of the *World Friendship* stood vivid

against the surrounding blue-green water of the Med. Nearly as vivid as the scattered silhouettes on the deck.

Everyone present recognized that those images were human beings.

Children.

"A group of terrorists have hijacked a friendly vessel. Communication has been nonexistent, with the exception of a single transmission to a ship of Greek registry at oh-nine-hundred."

Lord slapped his legs with the pointer as Sacrette asked flatly, "What are their demands?"

"Demands have not been given at this point." Lord nodded at the UN delegation sitting in the front row. "With one exception. Instructions were issued demanding the presence of a UN delegation. The delegation will be helped to a rendezvous point at seventeen-hundred."

"For what purpose?" Stennard asked.

"The UN will be carrying the ball since the cruise is under their sanction. The *Valiant* has been designated as the temporary command center. The UN has dispatched a hostage-negotiation team. We are at their disposal, and will conduct ourselves accordingly."

Sacrette sighed heavily. "In other words, no one is going to do a damn thing."

Lord looked sternly at the men. "Not exactly. The Pentagon has given us the yellow flag."

A low groan echoed from the rows of leather chairs.

Lord held up his hands, as though fending off an aggressor. "I know. It's not what we want. But at least it's something. State—and the Pentagon—have ordered an operational plan of action to be in place for immediate implementation should we be given the go."

Sacrette pointed to the screen. The blips indicating

the carrier and that of the sailing vessel were now on opposite ends of Crete. "That's a long stretch of water between the *Valiant* and the *Friendship*, Captain."

Captain Lord nodded in agreement to the CAG. He checked his watch. "The *Friendship* is a sailing vessel. It's currently making fifteen knots into a headwind. We're at flank speed, twice that of the *Friendship*. We will be within thirty miles of her location by twenty-two-hundred."

"Where's the ship going, Captain?" asked Stennard.

The captain folded his hands behind his back. "If the ship maintains its present course . . . it should arrive in Tobruk within thirty-six hours."

Libya!

The implication cracked like thunder.

Sacrette grinned. He relished any opportunity to go fangs out with the Colonel's Cookies, as Qaddafi's pilots were known.

Sensing the renewed enthusiasm generating through the ready room, Captain Lord spoke cautiously, "Gentlemen, we know where they're going. That's the easy part. It's obvious Qaddafi will give them asylum. Which brings us to the more challenging aspect . . . launching a full-scale rescue mission without stirring up an international incident."

"With who, Captain? The terrs . . . or Qaddafi!" asked Domino.

Laughter broke out.

"Hell, Captain, that's like telling us to make an omelet without breaking any eggs," added Blade, who was sitting at the rear of the room.

The captain shook his head. "Not the Libyans." He paused, pointing to a string of blips near the Libyan coast. "As you're aware, a Soviet naval battle group is conducting maneuvers off the coast of Libya. Extreme caution must be exercised to avoid any acts the Sovs might construe as intimidating. However, contingencies will be drawn up to include two possibilities. A sea-rescue mission. A hostile territory mission."

Sacrette shifted uncomfortably in his chair. He pointed at the blip on the screen indicating the sailing vessel. "Rescue at sea would be tricky . . . but easier than in Libya. Once they reach Tobruk there's no way of guaranteeing any kind of advantage. Not to mention the fact that the entire Libyan military will back the terrorists' play."

Lord slapped the pointer into the palm of his hand. "Our hands are tied, gentlemen. We will devise an operational plan of action for the Pentagon and await further instructions." The captain pointed to Sacrette. "Commander, VFA-101 will proceed to Alert Five. I want two birds on the deck. Ready to launch."

"What about standard patrol?" Sacrette asked. He was becoming uneasy as the captain's meaning began to grow like a festering boil.

Glancing at the faces of the pilots, Lord appeared in pain as he announced, "All air ops are suspended until further notice. Except to protect the battle group. Which, I doubt, will be threatened."

"Why, Captain?" Sacrette was leaning forward, nearly standing from his chair.

"The State Department is concerned air activity in the area might provoke the Russians."

Silence fell onto the ready room.

Domino was the first to voice what each man believed to be the truth. "Christ almighty, Captain. That smells a little too Russian."

"Explain yourself, Lt. Commander." Lord's eyes narrowed into two fiery shafts.

Domino spoke directly to the point. "The timing's a little too damned coincidental, sir. First, a group of terrorists hijack a UN sailing ship. Second, the ship is reported to be sailing toward Tobruk, where a Soviet battle group happens to be conducting maneuvers off the coast of Libya. To make matters worse, we're expected to ground our aircraft in order not to provoke the Ruskies."

"Get to the point, Lt. Commander," Lord's voice snapped.

Domino glanced at the UN delegation, whose suspicious looks tempered his words. "My point is . . . Qaddafi's behind every terrorist operation in this part of the world. And, the Russians back Qaddafi." He shook his head incredulously. "We've got the ship in the open. Once it hits Libyan waters they're home free, under a Soviet cover. If we don't move now . . . we won't have a move."

"Captain Lord, Domino is suggesting the Russians may be behind the entire operation." Stennard spoke bluntly, not caring what the UN negotiators thought.

Lord shook his head. "That would seem highly improbable." Motioning the West German representative to stand, the captain said, "Herr Friedrich, would you care to explain."

Friedrich stood. "Gentlemen, I assure you the Soviet Union is cooperating one thousand percent in this matter." Raising his arm, Friedrich signaled the yeoman standing guard at the back of the ready room.

As the door opened, a uniformed officer marched sharply down the aisle. Nearing the podium, the officer paused arrogantly, allowing everyone present a slow, agonizing perusal.

A sudden, uncomprehending gasp came from the men sitting in the brown leather chairs.

Sacrette looked hurriedly at Zena. What he saw on her face was not surprise; rather, she seemed to be apologizing.

"Gentlemen," Friedrich's voice rose above the clamor. "I would like to present the helicopter pilot who flew our delegation to your carrier. Major Sergei Zuberov, naval air attache to the Soviet embassy in Athens."

Sacrette's eyes turned molten with fury, his face twisting into a mask of unconcealable rage.

"Gentlemen." Lord's voice carried a twinge of defeat. "The terrorists' demands included an unexpected codicil." Staring spitefully at the Russian, Lord added, "Whoever the terrorists might be, they have demanded the negotiation team be delivered to the *Friendship* by helo. A Soviet helo. Flown by a Soviet pilot."

Realizing he would add insult to injury, Captain Lord spoke swiftly, his words coming so fast Sacrette failed initially to grasp their meaning.

"Commander Sacrette, you will accompany the negotiators to the rendezvous point." When Sacrette didn't respond, Lord asked again, "Is that understood, Commander?"

Sacrette heard nothing, except the voice of a young naval flight officer, his A-7 Corsair in flames, trying to eject over Beirut. The voice had haunted Sacrette since the young pilot's death.

As did the second voice, taunting the American flier before firing a missile into his disabled aircraft.

Naval Intelligence later confirmed that the voice was

that of a Soviet pilot attached in an advisory capacity to the Syrian air force.

The voice of Major Sergei Zuberov.

The eagle Boulton Sacrette constantly encountered in his dreams!

7

"JEMAL! JEMAL!" THE URGENCY IN RASHID'S VOICE pulled the dozing Jemal through the groggy haze clouding his brain.

Slowly the terrorist rose from the bunk, trying in vain to smooth the fatigue from his aching eyes.

He checked his watch. 1700.

Nearly two days had passed without the refreshment of sleep.

Opening the cabin door, Jemal found the excited Ashbal youth pointing wild-eyed toward the upper deck.

Jemal planted a firm hand on the boy's shoulder, squeezing Rashid's neck muscle until the boy winced in pain. "What is happening? You sound like a frightened old woman."

Pointing again, Rashid blurted excitedly, "They are coming!"

Pushing his way past the Ashbal, Jemal darted through the narrow corridor to a hatchway. Within seconds he was standing on the quarterdeck where the steady beat and thump of helicopter blades spoiled the air.

Awad and Meheisi knelt at the railing, their weapons trained outward to the Mediterranean.

Rushing to Jemal's side, Rashid thrust his AK-47 to the horizon, where a dark object appeared against the fading sky.

"Helicopter!" Rashid said bluntly.

A wicked smile cut across Jemal's face. Raising binoculars to his eyes, he observed the approach of a helicopter. "The markings are Soviet."

"Gunship?" asked Rashid.

Jemal shook his head sharply. "No, little brother. But where one vulture soars, others may lurk nearby." Turning slowly, he scanned the full 360-degree range surrounding the *Friendship*. He saw nothing but open water.

Jemal removed a small transmitter from his belt. With a quick jerk he extended a short antenna. Two buttons controlled the detonating device. A white button for arming. A red button for detonating.

Kahlil's pulse quickened. Glancing along the deck, his eyes slowly examined the ten yellow barrels transferred from the *Helenas* after the taking of the *Friendship*.

Each barrel contained 200 kilos of Chezh Symtex, giving the terrorists enough destructive force to vaporize the *Friendship* in a whisper.

Jemal pressed the white button. "Bring the woman," he ordered.

8

BOULTON SACRETTE LEANED THROUGH THE OPEN door of the Soviet Mil-26 helicopter, his thoughts drifting from the pilot to the dark figures rushing around on the deck of the *World Friendship*.

For both entities he felt nothing but loathing, and given the look on his face, which the propwash pushed into a twisted, ghoulish mask, he appeared ready to treat both with equal severity.

First things first, he reminded himself. Then... other matters can be settled. He pointed to the sailing ship. "She's making about fifteen knots. South by southwest."

Zena leaned through the door. Her red hair was pushed back by the propwash. Her face was bronze, except for a narrow band of white skin on her forehead, where her bangs had blocked the hot Israeli sun. Her lips moved slowly as she counted the figures on deck; those carrying weapons. "I count four."

Sacrette saw a figure dashing along the deck, toward the bowsprit.

Reaching the forwardmost point of the *Friendship*, the man jutted his arm toward the helicopter.

"What's he doing?" Sacrette asked Zena.

Raising her binoculars to the lone figure standing at the bowsprit, Zena saw the fanatical face, recognized the man, then the object in his hand. When Jemal pointed at the yellow barrels, Zena's face became ashen.

Zena's peculiar expression was not lost on Sacrette. "What do you see?"

Zena leaned into Sacrette's ear, shouting, "Mohammad Abu Jemal! He's pointing a detonator. I suspect the ship is rigged with explosives."

Unable to hear over the noise of the rotors, Sacrette closed the door, then asked again, "Who?"

The engine noise diminished, allowing Zena to explain. "Mohammad Abu Jemal. He's Palestinian. The ship is rigged with explosives."

Sacrette wasn't surprised. "It figures. Only the PLO could feel secure making a run for Libya."

Zena handed Sacrette the binoculars. "Look closer. At the terrorists kneeling along the rail. They are more than PLO."

Sacrette shrugged, wondering why she thought the terrorists so special. To him, a terrorist was a terrorist. Then he scanned the deck, and understood. His mouth went dry. "Christ," he muttered. "They're kids!"

Zena nodded. "Ashbal. Children soldiers trained to carry on the war against Israel in the next generation."

Sacrette released a long sigh. "Brilliant move on their part."

"Yes. The use of children terrorists adds a new dimension to the negotiations. It strengthens their position."

Sacrette agreed, "Strengthens! They've got a pat hand. I doubt our government will want to launch an attack on a band of children. Terrorists, or not. Not after what's been happening in Gaza. The world press would have a goddamned field day."

The voice of Zuberov interrupted, "Commander Sacrette, there's activity on the deck."

9

ELAINE WINTERS WALKED STIFFLY, HER EARS ANTIC-
ipating any sound that might tell her what was happening. She was blindfolded, as she had been since the
hijacking, yet her bare feet told her she was passing
through the salon, the only part of the ship that was
carpeted.

Pausing, she listened for the children; she heard
nothing. A sharp pain bit at her side.

"Move!" ordered Layla, prodding the barrel of her
AK-47 into the chaperone's ribs.

"Where are the children?" Elaine demanded.

"They are well," was the only response.

Elaine felt the opening of a door, then started to
protest when the faint roar of an approaching helicopter
seeped into the heavy silence. As she was shoved through
the door, she felt another stab from the prodding rifle.
She stumbled, then fell hard to the floor.

"I don't know how you expect me to walk if I can't
see! Please. Remove the blindfold." She waited anx-
iously. Finally, a tugging at her head, and the darkness
fell away, replaced by the light seeping through the port-
holes of the after section that was the boys' sleeping
quarters.

She pulled herself upright, moving slowly to allow her eyes time to adjust. As she glanced around, the stark emptiness of the bay struck her with a cold reality. The bunks were empty, stripped of their mattresses and beddings.

"Oh, God," she whispered softly. She didn't need to ask further questions. The emptiness confirmed the gnawing fear that had begun shortly after she was locked in her cabin.

Layla prodded again, pushing her along until she climbed the steps to the main deck, where Rashid hurried her toward the bowsprit.

The air was electric. From behind their rifles, the Ashbal glanced only momentarily at the chaperone, then returned their gaze to the helo hovering thirty feet off the port bow.

Standing at the bowsprit, Jemal was holding a board toward the helo. Scrawled on the board was the message:

SEND ONE PERSON ABOARD!

Elaine watched breathlessly as a figure emerged from the open door of the helo.

"Hook up!" Sacrette shouted to Zena. He was gripping the hook joined to the exterior cable winch. He pointed to the carabiner attached to the harness she was wearing.

Standing in the door, Zena reached for the hook. The roar of the twin Lotarev D-136 turboshaft engines was deafening, pulsating with such intensity Zena thought her eardrums would explode.

Suddenly the helo yawwed. Sacrette fell backward, his hand still extended toward Zena, whose face froze as she felt the sickening sensation of momentary weight-lessness.

Zena disappeared; the hook dangled loosely in the propwash.

"Jesus!" Sacrette blurted, darting into the doorway. Below, he could see Zena was a blur against the blue water.

"Fuck me!" he groaned as he stepped into the open air.

Moments before Sacrette hit the water, he caught sight of Zena making impact.

A white, foaming geyser shot straight up, engulfing Sacrette as he fell through the exploding upshot of sea-water. He hit the surface clean, his body tight, hands cupped over his groin. He allowed himself to sink, then, looking up, he spotted Zena floating above him, appar-ently unconscious.

He kicked hard, driving his hands through the water, pulling himself closer in a furious race against time. Reaching her, he gripped her hand, then kicked for the surface.

Seconds later, with Zena in tow, Boulton Sacrette surfaced beside the sailing ship.

He looked up and felt his features turn to stone. From the railing, the muzzles of four rifles offered a men-acing welcome.

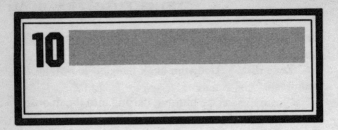

10

SACRETTE'S WRISTS BURNED FROM THE ROPES; EACH effort to free himself brought another stinging reminder that he had enjoyed better days. He was sitting upright, blindfolded, with his feet and hands bound. A rope ran from his ankles to his neck, choking him with every move.

"Kids, my ass!" he mumbled. "Did you see the look on that girl's face when she was tying my hands? She looked like she could breathe fire!"

Sitting beside him, Zena said nothing. She tried to move, but the reward of pain was too unbearable. Her body felt as though it were made of jelly; a sharp, burning sensation ran in relays from her spine to her feet, signaling her brain that her back was sprained from the fall.

At least, she thought somewhat gratefully, she was alive. For how long was yet to be decided.

Sacrette twisted again; a sharp stab tore at his ribcage.

"Bastards," he breathed heavily at the movement hovering over him.

The terrorist, the one called Awad, had inflicted a rifle thrust with each of Sacrette's movements.

Sacrette turned his head toward him. He wanted to

curse, but the rope biting his neck reminded him prudence and diplomacy were the order of the moment. "Come on, kid. Get your boss over here. We have to talk about this situation." Sacrette waited for a reply.

None came.

Awad shifted his attention to Jemal, who was storming about the deck, raging at Elaine Winters, whom he dragged at his side by the hair on her head.

Awad, a skinny, gangling boy of twelve, knew better than to interrupt Jemal. He chose instead to raise his rifle; he pointed at the helicopter hovering overhead.

"I should kill you! All of you!" Jemal raged. Pushing Elaine to the deck, he rushed to Zena. Grabbing her arms, he pulled her upright. Pain raced through her body. It took all her strength to remain conscious.

"Come on, Chief!" Sacrette blurted. "This isn't getting us anywhere. For Christ's sake! You know this wasn't planned." Reason with the man, Sacrette reminded himself. Reason. "The lady sitting beside me is one of the negotiators from the UN. The helo is Soviet. We've done everything you've asked. She's been injured. If she doesn't receive medical attention she could die. Where will you be then? You'll be finished before you get started."

Jemal's fingers tore at the blindfold covering Sacrette's eyes. A suspicious look spread across his face. One finger pointed at the helo. "The helicopter is Russian?"

Sacrette nodded; the rope cut at his neck.

Jemal pointed at Zena. "She is from the UN? The one I requested?"

"One of three sent by the United Nations to hear your demands, as you instructed."

Jemal tapped Sacrette's chest. "You are not Russian. Who are you? American?"

Fearing his uniform might be spotted by the terrorists, Sacrette had worn civilian clothes. Jeans. Sneakers. His identity was aboard the *Valiant*.

"Canadian. I'm with the UN delegation," Sacrette lied.

Jemal nodded knowingly. "Yes. Canadian. I have been to Canada. What city are you from?"

Sacrette didn't miss a beat. "Winnipeg." His grandfather had been born in Winnipeg.

"What is your nation's song?"

Sacrette looked confused. "What?"

"The song. The song. What is Canada's song?" He was growing impatient.

Sacrette thought for a moment. "Song? You mean anthem?"

"Yes. Anthem."

"'O Canada.'"

"Sing it."

"Wha—?" Sacrette saw Jemal's hand flash from his side. The barrel of a pistol pressed against the fighter pilot's temple.

"Sing it! Or die. If you're Canadian, you'll sing the song. If you don't know the song . . . you're American."

Sacrette swallowed; his lips were dry, his throat cracking. His mind flashed back over the years, to his grandfather, who had insisted young Boulton Sacrette learn the national anthem of his ancestors. How he hated having to learn two anthems. Until now, as the words began to roll from his mouth.

An explosion of laughter erupted from the Ashbal, who were quickly silenced by a hateful leer from Jemal.

Sacrette completed the first part, in English; then,

the second part, in French, as it is traditionally done in Canada. When finished, he waited for Jemal's decision.

Jemal lowered the pistol. "You are Canadian," was all he said.

Sacrette released a long sigh. Looking down at Zena, he realized she was getting worse. "My associate needs medical attention. We are here to negotiate. Let me put her aboard the helicopter, then you can give me your demands."

Jemal gave this a moment's thought. His head shook vigorously. "No." He looked up at the helicopter. "What frequency is the helicopter receiving on?"

Sacrette recalled the preflight briefing. "One-twenty-one-point-five. The international emergency frequency."

Jemal went to the radio at the helm. He hurriedly turned on the radio, punched in the frequency, then issued his orders to the pilot.

Sacrette heard Zuberov's husky voice respond.

The helicopter moved over the ship; looking up, Sacrette could see one of the crew lowering the winch cable hook.

Realizing what was about to happen made Sacrette's stomach tighten; not for himself, but for Zena.

Jemal took a knife and cut the rope running from Sacrette's feet to his neck. When the cable was lowered to the deck, Meheisi grabbed the hook and pulled it to Jemal.

His face wore a peculiar glow, as though he might know from experience what was planned.

Jemal ran the hook through Sacrette's legs; then through Zena's, looping the hook around the cable after both were connected. Looking up at the pilot, Jemal motioned the helicopter upward.

Slowly, the two bodies were hoisted off the deck.

Hanging upside down, Sacrette felt the blood begin running to his head. His brain throbbed with the fury of a locomotive. Looking at Zena, he saw her face bulge, then the light faded from her eyes as unconsciousness took hold.

Jemal reached into his pocket. He removed an envelope. He pried Sacrette's mouth open, then shoved the envelope into his mouth.

Clamping Sacrette's mouth shut, Jemal leaned and shouted over the roar of the helicopter. "These are my demands. Do not drop the envelope, Canada. Otherwise, you won't know the price for retrieving your precious children."

Sacrette looked at Elaine Winters; she appeared frozen with terror. He felt something in her eyes. She was trying to speak but there were no words.

A storm was raging in Sacrette's head; his pulse sounded like the tolling of bells.

Elaine was speaking now; shouting, but he couldn't hear. He saw Jemal's sudden movement toward the chaperone. She broke away, trying frantically to say something important enough to risk retribution. As she neared, there was another explosion.

The explosion came from beyond Elaine.

Elaine Winters suddenly straightened. Her jaw went slack; she twirled like a drunken ballerina, falling, spinning, and with each revolution Sacrette saw two holes become bright with crimson.

Bullet holes!

She fell to the deck beneath his head. Still trying to speak, her mouth moved. Looking down, Sacrette tried to read her lips, but he was himself drifting into a cocoon of silence, woven by the pressure in his brain.

Her hand came up. Another explosion.

Her body lay limp, her hand still reaching.

The roar of the helicopter filled the air as Zuberov lifted off hurriedly.

Sacrette felt the sensation of flight. He was again in the clouds, in pursuit of the eagle. No. *Flown by the eagle!*

He wanted to curse. To scream. To kill!

He could do nothing, except clench his teeth with all his strength.

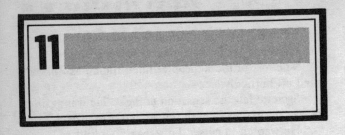

11

REGAINING CONSCIOUSNESS ON THE FLOOR OF THE Soviet helo, Sacrette felt the wheels of the Mil-26 touch the flight deck of the *Valiant*. Sitting in a webbed seat nearby, a blue-eyed Soviet crewman held Zena in his arms. For a moment, Sacrette was touched by the scene; then his eyes found the back of Zuberov's helmet, and nothing but fury stormed through his senses.

He tried to rise, but the numbness in his legs persisted, driving his body back to the deck. The crewman reached to calm him, but received nothing but the hard edge of Sacrette's hand across his forearm as payment.

"Get your fucking hands off me!" Sacrette breathed heavily.

By the time the rotor blades settled, a medical crew from the BDU was inside the Mil. Zena was carefully strapped to a stretcher; Sacrette refused assistance once he was helped onto the flight deck.

Feeling sensation return to his legs, Sacrette started back inside the Mil. He found Zuberov sitting in the cockpit. Oddly, the Russian appeared to be waiting.

"You bastard!" Sacrette shouted. "You could have killed us!"

Zuberov shook his head. "On the contrary, Commander. I could have let you get killed. Which, in view of your poor manners, might not have been a bad choice. I detest poor manners. Especially from an officer."

"As do I!" A voice cut through the air; a voice Sacrette would have recognized in a thunderstorm.

Captain Lord moved forward, his tall frame bent inside the fuselage of the Mil. "Commander. I believe you owe Major Zuberov an apology."

Sacrette's French-Canadian blood coursed furiously; his gray eyes, normally clear, were speckled with hatred.

"Now," Lord repeated firmly.

"If the captain orders."

"The captain so orders, Commander."

Sacrette nodded curtly at Zuberov. "My apologies, Major."

Lord glanced to Zuberov; the Russian nodded curtly. Looking at Sacrette, Lord asked, "Can you walk?"

"Walk! I can run! I can fly! That son of a bitch murdered that woman in cold blood, Captain. Cold fucking blood!"

"Yes. Major Zuberov gave us a grisly description of what happened once Miss Nesher fell. I don't know whether to commend or condemn you, Commander. That was a very brave act on your part."

"My thoughts, precisely," added Zuberov. "It took extraordinary courage." He shifted somewhat uncomfortably. "If I may, I'd like to apologize to Commander Sacrette for the misinterpretation. I was ordered by the terrorists to depart immediately. Had I not complied, I'm certain Miss Nesher and Commander Sacrette would have suffered the same fate as the chaperone."

"Christ," Sacrette mumbled, knowing it was the truth. What hurt most, he realized, was owing his life to

Zuberov. Suddenly that thought dissolved and his face slackened. Patting his shirt pockets, then pants, he realized something was missing.

"Is this what you're looking for, Commander?" Zuberov was holding the envelope that had been shoved into Sacrette's mouth by Jemal. His teeth marks etched the paper.

Lord took the envelope and, quickly reading the contents, looked at Sacrette with complete astonishment. "They must be insane!"

He handed the letter to Sacrette, who read the demands. Releasing a long, high-pitched whistle, Sacrette agreed, adding, "There's no way they'll go for this, Captain. No way in hell."

"May I see, Captain?" Zuberov asked.

"I'll save you the trouble, Major. In a nutshell, the terrorists claim to be Palestinian. They have issued four demands that must be met before they will release the children. First, the complete withdrawal of all Israeli security forces from the Gaza Strip. Second, the repatriation to Gaza of all Palestinians deported by the Israeli government. Third, that reparations be paid to all Palestinian citizens whose homes, businesses, and properties have been confiscated or destroyed. Fourth, and certainly not least, that the State of Israel agree to immediate UN-supervised negotiations with Palestinian representatives to establish a Palestinian homeland within the territorial borders of Israel, including the occupied territories."

Sacrette shook his head. "Not in this life, Captain. There's no way the Israelis will go for their demands. Kids or no kids."

Kids!

"Christ!" Sacrette added. "They are the terrorists!"

Lord looked confused. "Kids?"

"Yes, sir. Mean little bastards, but kids nonetheless. We counted four. I'm sure there're more below guarding the hostages. They're armed, deadly, and judging from their seamanship, they're pretty damn capable sailors."

"There was a man; the one who killed the woman," Zuberov added.

Sacrette thought. "He appeared to be the honcho. Zena said his name was Mohammad Abu Jemal." Sacrette shook his head earnestly. "He's the bastard I want in my gunsights."

Tapping the demand letter methodically, Lord appeared deep in thought. Sacrette sensed that the captain's concern was not only for the children hostages, but for the children terrorists as well. He could see that it was another of those moments when Lord regretted being a battle group commander.

"Anything else?" His voice was rock solid, devoid of the despair reflected in his face.

Sacrette thought; the haze from the blood filling his brain had cleared. Suddenly he recalled a small black box.

"The ship is rigged with explosives. The one called Jemal was carrying an electronic detonating device."

Zuberov added to the discussion. "I counted ten yellow barrels on the deck. Could they have been filled with demolitions?"

Lord thought for a moment. "Let's get this information to CINCLANT. We'll wait for their response." Glancing at Zuberov, Lord offered the Russian his hand. "Thank you, Major Zuberov. I suggest you return to Athens."

Zuberov shook his head slowly. "I am to report

aboard the Soviet carrier *Kiev*. May I request some fuel for my flight."

Lord quickly pictured the schematic of the Mediterranean map in the CIC; he saw the twelve red flashing lights indicating the Soviet battle group outside the Gulf of Sidra. "Request granted. Please extend my best wishes to Admiral Sholton aboard the *Kiev*."

Zuberov offered his hand to Sacrette. "Perhaps another time we can settle our differences, Commander Sacrette. For the moment, if we can't be friends, perhaps we can be professionals."

Their eyes joined for a long moment. Sacrette saw the same burning intensity in the Soviet pilot he knew burned in himself. Friendship? Never, he thought.

Professionals? Sacrette took the Russian's hand.

Before he released his grip, a strangeness enveloped Sacrette; something seemed to be radiating from the Russian. "Tell me, Major Zuberov . . . do you ever have a strange dream?"

The color drained from the Russian's face, as did the strength from his grip. He nodded. "Yes, Commander Sacrette."

Sacrette winked at Zuberov. "Until that day, I guess we'll just have to meet in our dreams."

DAY TWO

12

0030.

BOULTON SACRETTE'S MIND REPLAYED THE EXECU-
tion of the chaperone as one of several orderlies buzzing
around the sick bay hoisted Zena's body onto a pillow
and retightened the tension on the traction device cap-
turing her to a stryker frame.

She was positioned head down, her arms hanging
limp.

Sitting in a chair pulled close to Zena, Sacrette raised
a hand and began massaging his face. The effort proved
futile. The images of the chaperone remained.

Again her body twisted; her mouth opened to speak.

He was tired. His body ached, but other than a few
bruises his pain was easily forgotten, overshadowed by
Zena, who had remained unconscious since being lifted
from the *Friendship*.

"You look like hell." Commander Ansel Holweigner, the ship's doctor, approached. A stethoscope dangled loosely from his neck.

"Thanks. I needed that." He looked at the stryker
holding Zena like a fly caught in a web. "How long does
she have to stay strapped to that medieval torture device?"

Holweigner glanced nonchalantly at a metal-covered

chart hanging at the end of the frame. "It looks uncomfortable. Frankly, it's miserable as hell. But the alternative would be unbearable. Her fall from the helo nearly ripped the spine from her pelvis." He shook his head in astonishment. "The resilience of the human anatomy never ceases to amaze me. I don't know how she survived that fall."

"She's one tough lady," Sacrette said softly, remembering their first meeting. "We met in Israel. The Israelis were considering replacement of the F-4 with our new F-18. Her husband, Yanni, was the commander of an Israeli fighter squadron." He let out a long sigh.

"Do I detect something fatal in this relationship?"

Sacrette perched his chin on his steepled fingers. "Yanni was killed six months later. A SAM missile destroyed his aircraft over the Golan Heights." Sacrette fell quiet; he could only stare at her swollen face.

"Christ." Holweigner rubbed his eyes; he looked tired. "When will all this craziness ever end?"

Sacrette shook his head. "I don't think it'll ever end, Doc. The world's hurtling along on a crazy merry-go-round of self-destruction, and all we can do is hold on tight. Or jump."

"Coming from you, I find that a rather unusual comment. Something of a step out of character."

"Why?"

Holweigner shrugged. "Considering what you do for a living. I guess I never thought of you as being a compassionate man. A man concerned about humanity. The fate of the world."

A thin smile seeped along Sacrette's mouth. "Well, Doc, maybe I don't always come off as the caring type. But I do care about the world. The people. I have to. Otherwise, I couldn't do what I do."

"I don't understand." Holweigner's voice carried a tinge of genuine incredulity.

"I'm a fighter jock. You think all I care about is the action. The action means the death of other people. I see it differently. To me, it's not the death of those I'm facing. It's the safety of those I'm serving. You see life in its totality. I have to narrow the field. Retain my focus. That keeps everything in perspective. And to a pilot, perspective is the key to survival. It's all so clear. There's no gray area."

Holweigner lit a walrus-tusk pipe. A long curl of blue smoke snaked up his face, forming a cloud around features that now appeared more understanding. "What you're saying is . . . you kill to save? Hmmm. That's an interesting dichotomy."

"Dichotomy? Not really. There's no contradiction. You do the same thing, Doc."

"How's that?"

"For example, triage. You separate those who have less chance of living from those who can survive."

"There's a difference. I do that in an emergency situation."

Sacrette smiled. "That's my point. So do I."

"But I don't create the situation."

Sacrette sat back heavily in the chair. "Neither do I. When I'm attacked, I respond. I kill to save. Whether it's my life I'm saving. My wingman's. Or the crew on a tanker cruising through the Persian Gulf."

Holweigner puffed methodically on his pipe; he appeared deep in thought. Finally, he said, "I must admit, you offer an interesting argument."

Sacrette stood. He touched Zena's hand. "Not an argument, Doc. Just explaining my perspective." Nodding at Zena, he added, "Her perspective is much the same. She's a good woman in a bad situation. She's learned to quit thinking about humanity as a whole, and began concentrating on that part of humanity she can best serve. Like I said, it narrows the field. And it allows her to at least accomplish something important. Even if it's only for a few."

"Sacrette, I've always thought of you as a John Wayne hellfighter. Now I see there's something of a philosopher lurking inside that wiry frame. It's refreshing to know."

Sacrette grinned. "Hell, Doc. I'm a fighter pilot. Nobody ever said it would be easy being great."

Holweigner laughed aloud and, checking his watch, ended the conversation by suggesting the obvious. "You better hit the sack. You look like death warmed over. Miss Nesher will sleep through the night. If there's any change . . . I'll let you know."

Sacrette suddenly realized he hadn't slept in two days; his fatigue was like a heavy fog rolling in from the sea. He leaned over and kissed Zena on the forehead, then swaggered out of the sick bay.

He needed sleep; moreover, he needed to think. There was only one place he could do both.

13

THE VFA-101 MAINTENANCE AREA LAY DEEP WITHIN the bowels of the *Valiant*.

Normally a brightly lit, noise-filled area during duty hours, the area now lay washed in the red of a security lamp burning from a bulkhead. Silent and foreboding, the area was shrouded in stillness, except for the gradual movement of the carrier plowing through the sea.

Near elevator three, fifteen sleek F-18s sat in uniform lines, their wheels chocked, wings folded vertically at the wing fold hinge lines, giving them the eerie appearance of inverted pterodactyls.

A thin shaft of light penetrated the cockpit of *Double Nuts*, framing Sacrette's face in soft red; the smell of fuel floated thinly in the air, a constant reminder of where he was. What he was.

Adjusting his legs, Sacrette leaned back in the seat; gripping the control stick, he closed his eyes, trying to remember. Trying to hear. He read her lips, but nothing was understood.

"Why?" he asked the darkness. "Why would she risk her life? What was she trying to say?"

Answers didn't come.

Again he replayed the sequence. Again nothing.

As he was starting to pull himself out of the cockpit, the clicking of shoes approached on the metal deck. Turning, he saw a figure approach from the shadows.

"Commander Sacrette." The voice of Captain Lord echoed through the maintenance area.

"Yes, sir," Sacrette replied, watching Captain Lord walk smartly toward *Double Nuts*.

Lord stopped beneath the folded wing; running his hand along the leading edge, he appeared to be caressing the metal. Momentarily, he looked up, drawn back to his reason for searching out the CAG.

"We have a message from CINCLANT." Lord held a computer message from the commander-in-chief of Atlantic operations.

Sacrette pulled himself up onto the headrest where he sat cross-legged beneath the opened canopy. "Are we going to quit playing games, sir? Or is it more of letting the bastards kick us around the Med?" There was no apology in the way he spoke; he didn't feel apologetic.

Lord looked up severely; his mouth tightened, and in the wash of red light, Sacrette saw him appear demonic. "I prefer to talk with my subordinates on an even footing, Commander." It was all he said. It was enough.

Sacrette stepped down the boarding ladder. Dropping onto the deck, he snapped to attention, saluted, then waited.

Lord nodded approvingly; his hand slipped into his pocket. He removed an envelope. Sacrette recognized the envelope. His teeth marks were indelibly etched into the paper.

Tapping the envelope, he said, "We've been ordered to condition Zulu."

"It's about fucking time!" Sacrette replied; he

seemed to loosen as the relief showed on his face. Condition Zulu was the action command for the battle group.

"I agree. Apparently, so do the Joint Chiefs."

"What changed their minds, Captain?"

Lord said nothing.

"Christ!" Sacrette muttered, reading the captain's silence. "The Israelis have already rejected the demands."

"The Israeli government held an emergency meeting of the Knesset less than two hours ago. All demands have been rejected. The Israelis are holding the UN responsible for the children. Which only worsened the situation."

"How could it get any worse?"

"The UN has disavowed all responsibility, claiming it's the Israelis who can ameliorate the situation."

"Putting the ball in the Israelis' court. Smart move."

"As a matter of fact, the UN delegation has departed. Rather reluctantly, I might add. Only Miss Nesher remains, and she'll be medevaced when she's able to be moved."

Lord folded the envelope, adding, "Red Cell Six has been alerted. They are en route from Coronado. The Pentagon has given the 'go' for the operation as soon as the team arrives."

"Deke Slattery's boys. Good. They're the best."

Sacrette had worked with the Red Cell teams in past operations, especially in the Persian Gulf. Composed of select teams from the Navy SEALs, the antiterrorist hostage-rescue unit was, in his opinion, the finest commando fighting force in the world. Red Cell Six was by far the finest of all the teams.

"What about the *Friendship*? Any information regarding the yellow barrels?"

"Yes. The CIA has received information that a ship-ment of Chezh Symtex turned up mysteriously missing from a Bulgarian freighter two weeks ago. The canisters were yellow. Each weighing two hundred kilos."

"Jesus!" Sacrette breathed. "Over four thousand pounds of explosives. You could sink twenty ships with that much demolitions. The terrorists that blew up Pan Am flight 103 used less than a pound."

"Suggesting the terrorists are more deadly than we might have thought."

At that moment, Sacrette looked up. The captain's yeoman was approaching. "Captain Lord, the sailing ves-sel has altered its course." He handed a piece of paper to Captain Lord. "It is now sailing along this coordinate."

Lord studied the coordinate; the course felt familiar. His mind flashed the schematic from the map in the CIC, where a dozen red lights burned off the coast of Libya. As he mentally transposed the course onto the schematic, the imaginary line intersected in the one area he had failed to consider. "Damn," was all he could say.

"Where is the ship going, Captain?" asked Sacrette.

Captain Lord stated flatly, "The ship is sailing di-rectly toward the Soviet battle group!"

Sacrette straightened. "What are your orders, sir?"

"What do you suggest?"

Sacrette grinned. "I suggest we launch one aircraft. By maintaining surveillance, they'll know we're around. Perhaps we can dissuade them from their current course."

Lord shook his head. "Too risky. The children might be harmed."

Sacrette pressed his point by stating the obvious, a reality the captain didn't seem eager to address. "Risky? It's all risk, Captain. They won't harm the hostages, not as long as we have something they want. We can't let that floating demolitions ship near the Soviet battle group."

There was a suggestion in Sacrette's words Lord recognized immediately. Were the *Friendship* to come toward the American battle group, he knew what he might be forced to do.

It was reasonable to assume the Soviet battle group commander would do the same.

"Permission granted. Maintain a hard deck of one thousand feet. Don't intimidate. Position yourself between the *Friendship* and the Soviet battle group."

Sacrette saluted. "Aye. Aye. Skipper."

He marched away briskly, glowing with the look of the wolf smelling the scent of his prey.

14

0600.

THE WHINE OF ELEVATOR THREE BROKE THE STILL-
ness of dawn, signaling the crew on the *Valiant* flight deck
to their stations.

Commander Boulton Sacrette watched from his
cockpit, gliding upward on the elevator from the darkness
into the thin traces of a purple morning.

As he had done a hundred times before, he sat
watching the brown-shirted plane captains guide his
F-18 toward catapult one. Nearing the cat, he was passed
off to the blue-shirted arrest and launch crew, who carefully guided the Hornet into takeoff position. Within
minutes the fighter's catapult launch arm was engaged
in the steam-powered shuttle, arming the Hornet in
launch tension.

In the cockpit, Sacrette wiped out the controls, running a quick aileron and rudder check, then fired the
engines.

Closing the canopy, Sacrette glanced at the launch
officer, whose hand dropped suddenly.

Sacrette saluted, then shoved the throttles into full
military power as the shuttle shot forward, giving the
Hornet an instantaneous ground speed of 140 knots!

Instantly, twenty transverse g's slammed Sacrette

and Munchy into their seats; at the catapult jump extension protruding a few feet beyond the *Valiant*'s bow, the Hornet shot upward, then dropped below the bow, momentarily disappearing from sight.

For the next heart-pounding two seconds, all eyes of the deck crew remained focused on that spot above the jump launch, waiting for the aircraft to appear.

Failure to appear meant only one thing: the deep six!

"Hang on, Munch," shouted Sacrette, pulling the nose up as the Hornet increased speed in the gravitational pull of ground effect.

The Hornet shot straight up, returning the breath to the deck crew, who clapped one another on the back, then watched as Sacrette disappeared against the rising sun.

15

FIFTEEN MINUTES LATER, SACRETTE CRUISED AT AN-
gel's eighteen where the morning sun burned majesti-
cally at the eastern rim of the Mediterranean, appearing
to drain the blue of the water to a concrete gray at the
horizon.

In the distance, Boulton Sacrette could distinguish
the single signature of a sailing ship gliding over the
surface, her sails filled, moving fast and clean on a down-
wind reach.

To the south, the loam-colored coast of Libya lay
dry and rugged beyond the pincher-shaped outline of the
Bay of Sidra.

"Look at her, Munch. She's laying off the Sov's
perimeter. Close enough to be a pain in the ass, but
hanging back just enough not to draw flies."

Munchy glanced out the cockpit. "Reminds me a
little of Russian roulette, if you'll pardon the pun."

Sacrette laughed good-naturedly. "Russian roulette?
Hey, not bad, Munch."

Munchy said nothing; instead, he pointed at the
Friendship. "She's changing course again, Thunder-

bolt. Better contact the boss. Tell him she's coming about."

Sacrette pressed the microphone button. "Home plate, this is Wolf One. The unfriendly is coming about to a heading of two-seven-zero." Sacrette leaned forward, his attention focused on the sprinkling of ships now lying south of the *Friendship*.

Twenty miles from the *Friendship*'s port beam, more signatures registered on the surface where the Soviet battle group plowed lazily, twelve ships maintaining a constant rotation around the high-value unit at the core of the group, the Minsk-class carrier *Kiev*.

"Wolf One, this is the Umpire. Request photo surveillance run. Maintain a hard deck at Angel's one." The voice of Captain Lord rang in Sacrette's ear.

"Roger, Umpire. Wolf One, going in for a picture tour."

Sacrette lowered the nose, gaining airspeed as *Double Nuts* shot through fifteen, then twelve, finally, through 10,000 feet, where he raised the nose slightly, bleeding off airspeed while breaking the descent.

The hard deck, the lowest Sacrette was cleared for descent, was reached in a matter of seconds. Holding at 1000, Sacrette eased back on the throttles while lowering wing flaps, allowing the Hornet to float through the sky at minimum controllable airspeed.

"Home Plate, have deck of vessel in sight."

"Cameras on, Wolf One."

"Roger," Sacrette replied, arming the reconnaissance cameras. "OK, baby. Smile, you're on candid camera." He pressed the camera activator switch.

From one thousand feet the *Friendship* appeared

small, too small for an accurate visual glimpse that would offer any detailed information. However, from where he sat, Sacrette could make out the distinct movement of several figures scurrying across the deck.

16

MOHAMMAD ABU JEMAL DRAGGED HEAVILY OFF A GAL-oise cigarette, letting the smoke drift from his mouth into his eyes.

Through the blue-gray smoke, the sleek outline of the F-18 Hornet appeared wrapped in a cloud.

As he shifted slightly to adjust the long metal tube balanced on his knees, surprise didn't register in his face; nor did it on the faces of the young Ashbal sitting around him in a semicircle.

Pointing, he drew the children's attention to the fighter, telling them, "The Americans wish to play games." He nodded severely, as though something anticipated was finally about to happen.

Overhead, the sky was punctuated with the steady grumble of the fighter; on the deck, there was silence, as the children watched Jemal raise the metal tube to his shoulder.

"The F-18 is called the Hornet," he told the Ashbal. "A Hornet is an insect with a vicious sting." Releasing the safety switch on the General Dynamics "Stinger" missile, he smoothed its metallic surface lovingly, as though stroking a woman. "Come my pretty, let us show the American Hornet your sting."

Raising the surface-to-air, shoulder-fired missile, Jemal sighted carefully; when the fighter eased into his sight zone, his finger closed around the trigger.

A thunderous roar filled the air as the launched heat-seeking 3.5 HE rocket shook the deck, then streaked upward; moments later, the rocket's white tail turned sharply, banking in pursuit of the only source of heat lying between the sea and the burning sun.

Wolf One!

17

"HOLY SHIT!" THE STUNNED VOICE OF A YOUNG RA-
dar technician echoed through the *Valiant* CIC. Standing
excitedly, he pointed at a fresh blip burning white against
the green field filling the radar scope.

Captain Lord stepped hurriedly to the screen. Without hesitating, he spoke quickly into the microphone.
"Wolf One. Bogey approaching from the deck."

Sacrette didn't hear the transmission. The cockpit
of his Hornet reverberated with the warning system's
shrill report of the approaching missile.

"The son of a bitch! He's caught us at MCA!" Still
flying at minimum controllable airspeed, Sacrette shouted
into his mouthpiece; his ears rang from the lock-on warning signal screeching through the cockpit.

"Hit it, Thunderbolt! Get us out of here. Get us
gone!" shouted Munchy, who was watching the blip
closely from their six o'clock position. Momentarily, his
dark eyes locked onto the screen; the blip was less than
a thousand meters from their tailpipes. "Shit," he said
softly, his voice calm, but resigned.

Shoving the throttles to Zone Five, Sacrette was
slammed into the cockpit seat as fifteen transverse g's
crushed against his chest. Helpless, he could only stare

hopefully at the HUD, where the digital airspeed indicator skipped through 300, then 400 knots.

"We're not going to make it, Munch!" Sacrette bellowed as a thought invaded the heaviness of his g-soaked brain.

A thought that offered their only hope for survival. Taking a deep breath, the VFA-101 commander ordered sharply, "Eject! Eject! On your call!"

Munchy couldn't believe his ears, although his instincts, honed to incredible sharpness, began reacting like a computer.

Head firm against the headrest. Chin elevated to ten degrees. Back and shoulders firm against the seat. Elbows and arms tucked to sides. Thighs shoved flat against the seat. Heels on the floor. Feet firm on the rudder pedals. Safety off!

Completing the checklist, the seat fully armed, Munchy reached between his knees, gripped the ejection handle, and, pulling up, initiated his first "loud exit."

The next 1.5 seconds introduced Munchy to the fear he had heard of, yet never experienced.

Sacrette had ejected previously; yet he knew being a veteran made little difference.

In a flash, the canopy separated; the cockpit became engulfed in a swirling, pulling tempest of hurricanelike windblast.

Pinned to his seat, Munchy suddenly shot skyward as the Martin-Baker ejection seat automatically initiated the catapult system, separating the seat from the aircraft, launching the tandem seat vertically beneath a momentary crush of nearly 200 g's!

A crush that momentarily masked the sickening sound of bones cracking in the fury.

Sacrette's eyes nearly popped from their orbits. Unable to fight the tremendous gravitational pull, he fell limp and lifeless. When the seat rockets fired, separating Thunderbolt Sacrette from his seat, consciousness had evaporated somewhere between catapult and canopy deployment.

Munchy was less fortunate. He felt the rockets fire, the seat separating as he waited for canopy deployment.

He felt nothing but the rapid acceleration of the plunge toward terminal velocity.

Now! God dammit! Open!

The herky-jerky fall continued. *Fuck me!* he thought, reaching for his last shot at seeing tomorrow.

A coldness swept through him after his first reach for the rip-cord handle on his parachute harness. Again he reached.

In the next instance his mind snapped as his arms refused to rise.

Hot, searing pain flooded from his broken arms into his fractured shoulders. *God!* his mind screamed. *Give me one good arm!*

Still connected to the ejection seat, Munchy hit the water with the force of a runaway locomotive, thundering through the surface at over 120 miles an hour.

His entry point was marked by a spewing geyser of water.

Seconds later, the smooth, placid surface returned, erasing all traces of disturbance.

Below, wrapped in a shroud of nylon, Naval Flight Officer Juan Mendiola sank to the waiting abyss, his mouth cracked slightly. A thin trail of bubbles issued slowly, then ceased, as the last of his life was expelled in the darkness of his watery tomb.

18

SACRETTE LAY ON HIS BACK, HIS FLOTATION VEST riding his body high in the water. His helmet was off, revealing swollen, punished eyes blackened by the ejection.

Through the salt water and pain, a ghostly apparition materialized, its white lines appearing sleek through the haziness of his impaired vision.

"Hey, American pilot!" a voice shouted. "You are very lucky. No! Not like your comrade!"

Sacrette's vision cleared enough to make out a familiar face.

Thirty feet from where he drifted, the *Friendship* cruised by quietly.

On the bowsprit, holding the spent tube of the Stinger, Jemal raised the murderous weapon in victory.

The *Friendship* sailed closer, turning slightly, until it was heading directly toward Sacrette.

Leaning out from the bowsprit, Jemal hooked Sacrette with a long pole, pulling him alongside the sailing ship. As he looked down, a scowl formed on the Palestinian's face; a scowl brought by recognition.

"Hey, American," his voice hissed. "You are my

Canadian friend. No!" He jabbed the pole; the gaff bit into Sacrette's neck.

Glancing at the sky, Jemal added insult to injury. "You seem to have trouble staying in the air, American. Why do you keep landing in the water?"

Bobbing beneath the bow, Sacrette raised his hand, beckoning to the Arab. "Why don't you come here and find out, Mohammad Abu Jemal." He seemed to delight in letting the terrorist know he knew his name.

Jemal didn't share the humor. From beneath his tank top, Jemal's hand filled with an automatic pistol.

Sacrette, realizing it was the end, used his only weapon.

"Go ahead, motherfucker! Take your best shot. You're good at killing helpless people!"

Jemal's face turned to stone. Holding the pole steady, he raised the pistol. He started to fire when he stopped. Lowering the pistol, he said, "Shooting you would be too easy. And an unnecessary waste of bullets. I will let Allah feast on your devil soul."

Deftly, Jemal twisted the gaff, ripping a hole in Sacrette's flotation vest. The sharp hiss of air filled the water around Sacrette.

Throwing off the gaff, Jemal laughed aloud, chiding Sacrette as the *Friendship* passed. "You will die slow. Swim for your life, American."

Wearing full flight suit, boots, parachute harness, speed jeans, and life vest filling with water, Sacrette's body began to sink. He was reminded of a pilot's worst fear: alone at sea without flotation!

Realizing he was wasting his strength on the surface, he chose the neutral buoyancy of the sea, where time would begin to count against him, but where movement was easier.

Taking a deep breath, he quit fighting for the surface, allowing his body to slide into the watery realm of inner space.

He fell motionless, except for a slight roll forward, rotating onto his stomach in a spread-eagled freefall to slow his rate of descent.

It was then that his mind roared the first lifesaving command: *"Come on! Move your ass."*

Instinctively, Thunderbolt snapped to the command.

Boots off. Unbuckle parachute harness. Release speed jeans. Keep the flight suit.

Nearly twenty seconds passed. He was still sinking, the pressure increasing at a half a pound per foot.

His boots were off!

At thirty feet, the stinging from the pressure squeezing his ears and sinuses was unbearable. Finally, the pain passed as his eustachian tubes and ethmoidal sinus cavity filled with blood.

He unbuckled the parachute harness!

At forty feet, his lungs were ready to collapse as the last of his air was turned into carbon dioxide.

He kicked off the speed jeans!

Kicking hard, he raced for the surface.

His legs ached, and for a moment he wished he had ditched his flight suit.

As he neared the surface, there was an angelic ring in his ears. His brain starved of oxygen, he saw the floating form of Munchy drifting above him, urging him to his grasp.

"Munchy!" he shouted, venting the last of the residual air from his throat and trachea.

Sacrette reached. Cold, bony fingers closed around his wrist. He looked, and wanted to scream as the distorted form of Munchy suddenly appeared black and evil.

With his last strength he tried to pull away, but the figure held firm, pulling him toward the surface, toward the face that sat wrapped in black behind what appeared to be a wall of glass.

It was then, with his brain feeding on carbon dioxide, his lungs filling with the putrid taste of seawater, that he succumbed to the overpowering strength of the looming figure in black.

19

"I GOT HIM!" SHOUTED FARNSWORTH, HANGING FROM a cable beneath a Sikorsky Sea Stallion. He wore a black wetsuit and diving mask.

Tightening his grip around Sacrette's waist, Diamonds Farnsworth motioned with a quick jerk of his head to the crewman standing inside the opened door of the Sea Stallion.

With funereal slowness, the cable towed the two men toward the waiting helo.

"Easy, Thunderbolt. Easy." Diamonds's imploring voice grew louder as Sacrette squirmed, trying to grab the black chief. "You're home, Thunderbolt. You're safe."

Sacrette sat up, choking, gagging, his arms flailing out at Diamonds, who quickly subdued the CAG with his powerful arms.

"Get us out of here," Diamonds ordered the pilot.

"What about the other aviator?" asked the crewman.

Before Diamonds could respond, Sacrette's broken voice answered solemnly, "He was still in the ejection seat when he hit the water. He's gone!"

20

A DEEP, VELVET COCOON OF DARKNESS SURROUNDED Sacrette, wrapping him in a world where he could see nothing but the images of the past hour.

The blip on the screen. The blurred sky as he was launched from *Double Nuts*. Mohammad Abu Jemal. Farnsworth.

The sequence ran from beginning to end, then repeated.

Suddenly a blinding shaft of light turned the darkness into an abstract etching of a spiderweb, as the capillaries in his eyeballs reflected off the black veil.

Holding a penlight, Doc Holweigner examined Sacrette's eyes, then slowly suggested, "We've got to quit meeting like this, Commander."

"Yeah," Sacrette answered sarcastically. "People might start to talk."

"The talk has already begun, Commander Sacrette." The voice of Captain Lord pealed from the darkness beyond the light.

"What do you mean?" Sacrette asked.

"Tell him, Doc."

Holweigner's heavy breathing punctuated the severity in Lord's command, making Sacrette feel uneasy.

"What's the problem, Doc?" Sacrette demanded.

The penlight went out. Momentarily, the darkness was chased from the sick bay by the overhead lights.

Holweigner looked away, telling Sacrette, "In the last twenty-four hours you've suffered unconsciousness twice. Near unconsciousness on a third occasion. Not to mention an inverted right eardrum."

Sacrette swallowed hard. He had flown too many years not to understand the doctor's meaning. "Did you find anything wrong? Broken capillaries? Brain damage?"

Holweigner placed the penlight in his pocket. "None. However, that's not to say you haven't suffered a concussion. That ejection would put most men in bed for a week."

"I don't need to be in bed. I'm fine."

"Fine?" Holweigner's voice carried a tinge of resentment. "You let me make that determination."

"Then make it! God dammit!" Sacrette's gray eyes were burning.

"The doc has suggested grounding you, Commander." Lord was standing with his arms folded; he appeared less than delighted after having spoken the words all pilots knew were the kiss of death.

"Grounded!"

"For forty-eight hours. Until we can do a CAT-scan, bloodwork. A full flight physical workup."

Sacrette stood up. He looked at himself. He was wearing a hospital gown and felt ridiculous. "No way. I won't be grounded. Not after losing my RIO and aircraft to that bastard."

"Another point to consider, Boulton." Lord stepped forward, taking command of the conversation. "You don't have an aircraft."

Sacrette shook his head. He had been around long

enough to know that every situation offered an alternative. "Get me one from the RAG at Rota, Spain. They can have one ferried here within two hours."

A thin smile moved Lord's mouth slightly.

Sacrette noted the change. "You've already sent for a replacement."

Lord threw up his hands. "The Replacement Aviation Group at Rota has a spare aircraft. An A-model F-18."

"Good. The A-model is a single-seater. I won't have to wait for a RIO." The pain of not having Munchy in the pit knifed through him.

"Not so fast, Boulton. The doc has to clear you for flight duty. He has a good point. You've been through hell the last couple of days. I'm not so sure you should be on flight status."

Sacrette ripped at the gown. He was standing butt naked in front of the Zulu Station battle group commander. "You can ground me, Captain. That's a decision you have to make. In which case, I'll make another decision. One that's final."

"What might that be, Commander?" Lord already knew the answer.

"You can expect my retirement papers on your desk within the hour."

Lord's face turned metallic. "I don't like threats."

Sacrette walked to the bulkhead door. Turning, he stared knowingly into Lord's eyes, telling him, "I'm not making a threat. I'm French-Canadian, remember? We don't make threats. We deal in promises. If you didn't know that . . . you wouldn't have sent for the backup aircraft."

Without waiting for a response, Sacrette closed the door, then walked bare-assed to his quarters.

Stepping into the shower stall, he turned the water to Zone Five hot, creating a cloud of steam. He leaned against the stall, allowing the hot water to soothe his muscles while wishing there was something he could take to ease the agony in his heart.

There was nothing. Nothing for the pain except retribution. And the need for that flashed a warning from the past.

A warning from his first CAG, who always recited, *"Never take it personal. We're in the business of killing and dying. Never take it personal. If you do, you lose perspective."*

After showering, he dressed quickly, then started to leave when he suddenly remembered something important.

Reaching into his closet, he removed a wooden box. Opening the box, he found six twisted Cuban cigars.

Placing one of the cigars in his pocket, he went through the door, his voice hissing.

"Not this time, Captain Lord. This time . . . it's very personal!"

21

1600.

SACRETTE HEARD THE INCOMING H-53 SEA STALLION from the bow of the *Valiant*, where he stood beside Farnsworth smoking a Cuban cigar.

Smoking was something Sacrette rarely did.

Something he did symbolically.

The cigar wasn't for him. Each puff of smoke brought a cherished memory. Each exhale reminded him of the good times, the closeness to people he'd lost.

It was Sacrette's way of saying good-bye.

Flicking ashes at the "eyes of the ship," the huge eyelets where the *Valiant*'s twin anchor chains traveled during raising and lowering of the anchors, Sacrette was lost in thought.

"The Red Cell team is here," Farnsworth said softly. His eyes were red; his face ashen, like the gray remnants of the cigar.

Sacrette glanced over his shoulder to the helipad. He watched without expression as the side doors of the Stallion opened.

Another old friend stepped onto the deck of the *Valiant*.

"One coming. One going," he said in a whisper,

noticing that the new arrival had spotted him and was making for the bow.

"What was that, Skipper?" asked Farnsworth. Receiving no answer, he saw the vacant look in Sacrette's eyes and let the question slide.

A thought tickled Sacrette's memory. "Remember that night in Lisbon? When Munchy talked those two Iowa schoolteachers into climbing into that whaling boat hanging from the ceiling of the Europa bar? They climbed right up and joined that little three-piece band."

Farnsworth chuckled. "What I remember is them taking off their clothes, and then wishing they were someplace else when the booze wore off!"

Sacrette knelt. "God dammit, Chief. He was just a kid."

One of Farnsworth's large hands rested gently on Sacrette's shoulder. With the other he slipped a bottle of Jack Daniel's Old Number Seven from inside his shirt. Offering the bottle to Sacrette, he said, "Here, Thunderbolt. Let's drink to what was. We can't do nothing about what can't ever be."

Sacrette took a long swig. He wiped his mouth as the new arrival stepped forward, his hand extended.

Sacrette took the hand. The hand was rough, like the face, which looked as though it was carved from wood. "Good to see you, Deke."

USMC Major Andrew "Deke" Slattery stood two inches taller than Sacrette. He was narrow through the hips, broad at the shoulders. He was dressed in camouflage utilities; a red baseball cap bearing his rank insignia and gold SEAL pin sat above his close-cropped hair. When he smiled, it was quick, but recognizable, like the suddenness of a muzzle flash.

"Boulton. I'm sorry," came the first words out of

the mouth of the Red Cell Six team leader. "I heard about your RIO."

Sacrette handed the wiry SEAL the bottle. Slattery hoisted the whiskey. "Semper Fi." He took a long, slow pull from the bottle, then handed the Number Seven to Farnsworth. "Chief. Good to see you're in on the play."

"Deke." They shook hands. "How're your boys doing? They ready for some rock 'n' roll?"

Again the muzzle flash smile. "They're always ready."

Farnsworth turned his attention to the Stallion; to the five remaining SEALs of Red Cell Six who were unloading their gear. "I see some new faces."

Slattery nodded proudly. "A few. And one old moss-back you might recognize." Raising his arm, he motioned for the team to assemble.

Sacrette watched them approach; their movements catlike, lean, as though they were gliding over the deck.

Farnsworth noted one SEAL in particular. The closer the black-skinned marine drew, the wider Farnsworth grinned. "You sweet son of a bitch! Who taught you everything you know?"

"My momma!" replied the Marine SEAL.

"Your momma! Like hell. You never had a momma! You wasn't nothing but a bone-head, slick-sleeve private I found under a rock one day."

Gunnery Sergeant Franklin "Gunny" Holden towered above Farnsworth as they embraced. Extending Farnsworth to arm's length, Gunny chided, "Diamonds, my man, I heard you was out of the Navy. As a matter of fact, I heard you was in a stateside nursing home."

Farnsworth cocked his head at Gunny. "I was. But I got bounced out on my ass!"

"Bounced out?" A devilish grin licked at Gunny's lips. "Why would they do that?"

"For eating too many nurses." Both men roared.

Sacrette couldn't help but laugh as the old friends walked off together.

Slattery introduced the remainder of the Red Cell team to Sacrette, who was impressed by the intensity in their eyes. They looked like they could chew nails for lunch and eat a brick for dessert.

Private Jesus "Tico" Madrid was a stout Mexican wearing a wire saw around his neck. Sacrette knew what the wire symbolized: All SEALs were experts in the use of a garrote.

Navy corpsman Francis "Doc" Jerome was the team medical specialist. A medical kit bag hung from one shoulder. From the other, attached to a shoulder strap, hung a long gun case.

Sacrette didn't ask. Instinctively, he knew Doc doubled as the team sniper expert.

Lance Corporal Sam Phillips was tall and wiry. On his forearm he wore a Sykes-Fairburn fighting knife. Across his back, he carried a crossbow. The silent killer.

The last was a sailor, Conrad "Starlight" Gunnison. Removing his sunglasses, his eyes were two clear, colorless pools.

Slattery motioned to Gunnison. "We call this one 'Starlight,'" Deke said proudly.

"Why's that?" Sacrette asked, feeling he already knew the answer.

"Starlight was born with a very rare eye condition. One that nearly kept him out of the Navy. Tell him what happened at your induction physical."

Starlight's slow Texas accent rolled out softly. "They weren't going to let me enlist until I told the eye doctor to turn out the lights. Then I read him the chart in the dark."

Sacrette was genuinely impressed. Looking at Slattery, he slowly measured this man; a man much like himself.

A man, in many aspects, his exact opposite.

Both were professionals. Each man understood combat, which meant they shared the secret of survival. Each knew the difference between an amateur and professional was based on one fundamental premise: A professional knew how to cut down the odds.

Odds cutting, and consistency. Cutting down the odds meant gaining the advantage. Consistency meant confidence. Providing each of the players a predictability the others could count on. Within the game plan, the players could count on their teammates being where they were supposed to be, when they were supposed to be.

In this way, they were both professionals. Only their outward demeanor drew distinct differences in their personalities. Personalities shaped by the type of men they were, the work they did, and, more importantly, by where they stood in the arena of combat.

Sacrette was colorful; arrogant. A fighter pilot shaped from a mold that seemed to demand a certain personality. At supersonic speed, he entered combat, fought instinctively, then returned to the carrier, often still under the influence of instinct.

Slattery was the opposite. Quiet. Cold. Deadly. He saw the enemy up close. The taste of their breath often remained for days.

The memories of their dying did not take on the form of a distant fireball. They remained up close and personal. Slattery was a calculating killer of men. Methodical. Often mechanical. He would know how many there were, where they were, and how long it would take to eliminate each obstacle along the path.

Two men. Two personalities. Both professional.

Without another word, Sacrette turned to Deke Slattery. "Come on, Deke, let's go tear them sons a bitches out a new ass!."

"My pleasure," replied Slattery.

DAY
THREE

22

0400.

THE STORM HAD COME WITHOUT WARNING, INTER-
vening with whipping, blinding fury, turning the Mediterranean into a swirling tempest that tested the
durability of the USS *Valiant* and the men assembled on
her deck.

"Either we're living wrong . . . or those fucking terrs
are living right. They've got everything going their way,
Thunderbolt." Farnsworth was standing on the boarding
ladder, shouting to the pilot over the perpetual howl of
a force three wind.

"Remember, Chief," Sacrette replied from the
cockpit of his single seat F-18A replacement Hornet,
"they've got God on their side. All we've got is righteous
indignation . . . and overwhelming firepower. I'll take the
firepower over God any day."

"God!" As Farnsworth looked up at the slanting
rain, there was disagreement in his face. "The devil's
more likely on their side, Thunderbolt."

"Devil. God. It doesn't make a damn bit of difference. As a matter of fact, I feel fine." In reality it was
a lie. Sacrette had been getting the short end of the deal
from the terrorists since he jumped from the Soviet helo
to rescue Zena.

Today, he intended to bring about a resounding change.

"You would," Farnsworth countered, wiping the rain from his eyes. Glancing over his shoulder, he gestured to the line of aircraft waiting behind Catapult Launch Station One. "I wonder how they feel?"

"They're VFA-101, Chief. The Fightin' Hornets!"

"Yeah, I know. 'Cold. Bold. And bad to the bone. Not a deck too short . . . a woman too hard . . . or an enemy that can't be brought from the sky.'"

Sacrette grinned at the VFA-101 motto. "You got it, Chief. Now, get down and let me and this high-stepping little lady spend some time together. We're about to go on our first blind date."

As suddenly as he had appeared, Farnsworth dissolved into the blackness shrouding the deck. As was customary, he stopped at each of the fifteen aircraft sitting on the deck, chatting a few moments with the pilots, who were waiting for the launch sequence to begin.

Sacrette was number one. Domino would be his Dash Two, second in the order. Sitting in the cockpit at Alert Five, buckled in, ready to launch within five minutes' notice, Sacrette familiarized himself with his new aircraft, which he fondly christened the *Crunch 'n' Munch*.

The cockpit was essentially the same as it had been in the F-18B, with the exception of the weapons systems, which he would have to operate while flying. There was more leg room, which was nice; but still, he couldn't shake the eerie feeling that someone was there. "This one's for you, Munchy," he said softly, feeling the presence of his dead RIO.

Then leaning back, he wiped out the images, allowing the adrenaline to flow like kerosene. In a matter of seconds, he was at high confidence. Gone was the fatigue, the memory of yesterday. He was waiting for the hunt to begin.

He was in his element. As were the other participants in Operation Valiant Rapier, the code name given the mission by Captain Lord.

23

0410.

MAJOR DEKE SLATTERY LEANED FROM THE WEBBED seat attached to the starboard wall of the Sea Stallion. His face, painted in camouflage, looked ghoulish beneath the spray of magenta light enveloping the interior. Glancing through the port window, he could barely see the whitecaps fifty feet below where the storm rocked the surface of the Med.

"Hell of a goddamned surprise, Major," Gunny cursed from his side.

Slattery chuckled. He knew the tough marine didn't like flying through rough weather. "It's perfect, Gunny. Just the cover we need for the insert."

Gunny adjusted the HALO parachute harness he wore over a single scuba cylinder. Sweat beaded on his forehead, running in tiny rivulets along his black features. "Perfect! My old lady's ass is perfect. This is pure bullshit! How are we supposed to find that ship in this mess?" His head jerked toward the outside of the helo.

"Satellite surveillance, Gunny. The satellite will feed the ship's coordinates to the CIC. Our pilot will be guided to that coordinate. That's where we'll vacate the premises." Slattery looked down the line of webbed seats, to the rest of the Red Cell Six team. All wore parachutes and scuba tanks over wetsuits. Their faces were painted in green, white, and yellow. In their laps, the men cradled Uzi submachine guns, the standard close-range weapon of choice used by the SEALs. Silencers protruded from the muzzles, adding a deadly touch to the wicked purpose of their design.

Gunny checked his watch. "Whatever you say, Deke. I just wish we would get it on. Man, my stomach feels like something inside is trying to get out."

"There is, Gunny." He nudged the Marine SEAL. "Pure fucking meanness. That's what's trying to get out."

"Yeah," Gunny replied in a deep baritone voice. "Semper Fi."

Slattery sat back; his eyes closed slightly. "Yeah," he whispered. "Semper Fi."

24

CAPTAIN ELROD LORD WORE THE LOOK OF A MAN caught between a rock and the deep blue sea. He wasn't a man given to questioning orders, or to reconsidering decisions he had made based on good judgment.

Now, he wasn't sure.

Leaning against the coaming of the bridge, he kept glancing from the wall clock to the flight deck. The bridge was bathed in red light, standard procedure during night running to protect night vision. Slowly, the second hand ticked off the seconds, each methodical tick a reminder that Operation Valiant Rapier was approaching jump off.

He wasn't a man given to prayer. He knew God was probably too busy to worry about several of his creatures trying to destroy other members of the same race. He figured he was alone, as had been the case since the Pentagon ordered the mission.

During the debriefing there had been no indication that a storm might intervene. Now that it had, Lord could only push forward, placing his trust in his plan, the men responsible for carrying out the plan, and the fact that the terrorists would have their hands full with the storm.

That fact, perhaps above all, might be the edge the battle group commander would need to bring Operation Valiant Rapier to a successful conclusion.

25

0430.

"*ALLAHU AKHBAR!*" MOHAMMAD ABU JEMAL SCREAMED at the sky. His face was wet from rain mixing with slick seawater, his features transformed into an evil cowl. He was leaning on one of the yellow barrels, shouting above the howling gale to his younger minions. "Allah, in his most divine grace and wisdom, has heard your prayers!"

Turning to the young Ashbal, who stood wide-eyed, clinging to the rigging, he saw that they appeared frozen with fear. "Hurry, my brothers." He told them, "You know what to do. Allah has given us the moment we've been waiting for! We must not fail."

Without hesitation, the young Ashbal slung their rifles and scurried to their positions, moving stiffly and uncertainly through the tempest raging over the deck of the *Friendship*.

Working in pairs, they obediently set about their task, ignoring the fear that only moments before had shaken them to their core.

At the foremast, Layla and Rashid stepped barefooted into the rigging and, against the force of the wind, the rain, and the fear of failure, pulled with all their strength toward the main royal topsail.

At the mainmast, Awad and Meheisi did the same, climbing until they reached the main skysail.

Aft of both teams, Jemal climbed the mizenmast, where he stood perched precariously on the shrouds beneath the topgallant.

Without waiting for a command, both teams simultaneously reached for the leather sheaths on their belts. Drawing razor-sharp wire-cutters, they cut the wire-rope buntlines connecting the sails to the yardarms, sending the canvas whipping ghostlike toward the raging sea.

In minutes the ship was naked of sail, its steerage all but dictated by the waves rolling along the surface.

They regrouped at the helm, where Jemal issued orders to the young Ashbal, who knew the next part of the mission would be the most difficult and, certainly, the most dangerous.

"Do you understand?" he asked.

They nodded; he appeared pleased. "Good. Go to your stations. Prepare yourselves. It will begin soon."

He watched the four children of Palestine race toward the bow, then turned to the business at hand.

His hands moved quickly, setting the directional gyro to the same heading as the magnetic compass, then pressed the SET button on the automatic pilot. Pressing the digital select switch, he tuned in the new course, as indicated by the digital numbers burning on the automatic pilot course indicator.

Pausing, he glanced at the deck, where the young Ashbal were now assembled beside their equipment.

A pleased look filled his face; then, as planned, he pressed the ON button.

He waited patiently. Then, gradually, like the early rumblings of an earthquake, he felt the deck begin to move. Finally, the bow began turning ever so slowly, pulling the *Friendship* onto a new course despite the punishing argument from the stormy current.

When the *Friendship* reached the desired heading, Jemal raised his hand in triumph, beckoning the children. "Time is now our enemy. Not the sea. Not the Americans. May Allah be with you all."

They kissed ceremoniously, as do all fedayeen before facing death, then turned into the raging wind sweeping the deck.

Minutes later, the deck lay empty, except for ten yellow barrels.

26

0500.

THE SKY ABOVE THE MEDITERRANEAN TURNED
charcoal gray, the morning barely recognizable, except
at Angel's eighteen, where VFA-101 flew a constant rotation around the coordinates that satellite surveillance
had designated as the course of the sailing vessel *World
Friendship*.

The sky overhead was blue, clear; in the distance,
the sun inched its way from darkness, forming a golden
crescent at the horizon.

To the west, stars were still visible in that single
moment where night gives way to day, but not without
reluctance.

Looking down, Sacrette shook his head in disgust.
A long, gray cloud bank smothered the sea with a thick
carpet that began at two hundred feet off the water, then
shot upward, building to a plateau at ten thousand feet.

"No relief for the weary," Sacrette said aloud, forgetting that no one was listening. Automatically, he
turned to the pit, which didn't exist in the F-18A, and
realized that since Viet Nam, this was the first mission
he'd flown without a rearseat weapons officer.

The flight was boring; except for the Cat Shot from
the catapult launch station aboard the *Valiant*.

Fly outbound for sixty seconds, execute a 180-degree turn. Repeat. Outbound. Repeat.

The radio traffic was quiet, except for the occasional sit-rep exchanges between the helo pilot and Home Plate, who had put Red Cell Six on hold, ordering the Sea Stallion pilot to gyro the *Friendship*'s position.

Noticing that there hadn't been any significant heading changes in the last fifteen minutes, Sacrette broke the silence, asking Home Plate, "Home Plate from Wolf One . . . What's the situation, Umpire? Do we still have a ball game? Or a rain delay?"

A long pause followed before Captain Lord replied, "Game still scheduled as planned. Fans having trouble finding a seat. Stay on the mound."

"Christ." Sacrette's voice was nothing more than a sigh. Glancing to Domino, who rode his three as Dash Two, Sacrette threw up his hands in resignation.

"Ah, yes," Domino's Brooklyn accent crackled over Sacrette's headset. "The exciting life of the fighter pilot."

Sacrette pointed below, to the deck. "Not as exciting as down there."

"Roger that," Domino came back. "That stuff's thick enough to cut with a knife."

"Thicker," the voice of Blade broke in. He was pulling onto Sacrette's nine o'clock wing position. "What are we supposed to be covering for, Thunderbolt? It wouldn't make sense for the Libs to venture this far out to escort the ship. Hell, man. We're two hundred miles from Qaddafiland."

Before Sacrette could respond, his radar screen lit up with no less than two dozen bogeys.

"Mother Carey's Chickens!" Blade cited the small birds known to fly near ships as a storm approached. "What in the hell is that? Am I seeing things, or do we have bogeys?"

"We've got beaucoup bogeys, Thunderbolt," Domino, staring at his radar scope, spoke hurriedly to the CAG.

Sacrette wasn't tuned to the intraship communication net. He was already on the horn to the *Valiant* CIC, and Captain Lord.

"We've got traffic, Home Plate. I count twelve . . . negative, fourteen bogeys, moving along a two-eighty heading at one-twenty. Over."

"Roger, the bogeys, Wolf One. Have received transmission from Soviet battle group. The bogeys are Soviet. Repeat. The bogeys are Soviet."

"What in the hell's going on, Home Plate? Are the Sovs friend or foe?" Thunderbolt demanded.

There was a hesitation. "Status uncertain. Remain on station. Will contact Soviet battle group for explanation."

The radio went silent.

Sacrette, not certain of anything except the fact that there were bogeys in the air, ordered the Fighting Hornets to battle stations.

"Let's be safe, and not sorry, gentlemen. Break for combat positions. Maintain acuteness on ROE. For those of you needing a reminder, the 'rules of engagement' require us not to fire unless we are certain to be fired upon. Do you copy. Over."

The Fighting Hornets checked in through the Dash Ones in each two-man formation. Seconds later, seven pairs of F-18s had taken combat positions at Angel's eighteen.

Watching the screen, Sacrette was puzzled by the

airspeed of the bogeys. "They must be flying at MCA," he said to Domino.

"Either minimum controllable airspeed, or they're not fighters," Domino replied.

Sacrette felt a tingling in his spine. "Jesus!" he spit, pressing the microphone button on the pole. "Home Plate, Wolf One requesting intercept and visual on bogeys. Over."

The hesitation from Home Plate was all Sacrette required to make a command decision. "Wolf One to Wolf Pack, dropping down for a visual. Domino, it's on your call up here."

Passing the wing command off to the exec, Sacrette lowered the F-18A Hornet's nose, and seconds later, the sleek fighter disappeared through the deep cloud bank covering the Mediterranean.

27

"YOU CAN FORGET THE ELEMENT OF SURPRISE, Major. Those bastards just flushed your operation down the shitter."

The Sea Stallion pilot was pointing through the windshield of the helo. Slattery knelt beside him, his face hardened as his eyes focused on the horizon where more than a dozen objects began to materialize off the starboard bow of the *World Friendship*.

"Damn!" Slattery clenched his fists, then relaxed, allowing the anger to run its course. "Let me have your ears." He removed the pilot's headset from the aviator's head without waiting for permission.

"Red Cell leader to Home Plate. We've got a problem, Captain." Slattery's eyes remained focused on the hovering objects that seemed to be standing still one hundred feet above the sea.

"Roger, Red Cell leader." In the CIC, Captain Lord began reading from a sheet of paper he was holding. "Red Cell leader and Wolf Pack leader, I have received a communiqué from the commander of the Soviet battle group. It reads as follows: 'Have taken necessary action to protect my battle group. Unfriendly vessel—*World Friendship*—has entered my perimeter. Have attempted to contact vessel. No response. *World Friendship* ordered to reverse course immediately. Further encroachment will be construed as hostile.'"

Sacrette's voice interrupted over the intercom in the CIC. "Wolf One to Umpire. Have bogeys in sight." Sacrette was flying an interdiction rotation around the *Friendship*, placing himself between the ship and the bogeys. He was so close to the surface, small geysers of water shot upward where his fighter's exhaust ricocheted off the sea. Close enough to the bogeys to realize the imminent threat now complicating the mission.

"What's the picture, Wolf One?" Umpire's steely voice demanded.

"We've got a herd of 'Devil's Chariots' hovering off the *Friendship*'s port bow. And I think they mean business," Sacrette replied.

"Are you sure, Wolf One," Umpire came back sharply.

"I'm staring in their eyes right now, Umpire. Waiting for one of the bastards to blink."

Through the canopy, Sacrette was watching the pilot of the lead bogey, who appeared to command the wing of fourteen Soviet Mil–24 Hind attack helicopters. Earning the nickname "Devil's Chariot" from the Afghan rebels, each Hind was armed with four deadly AT-6 Spiral air-to-ground missiles.

"There will be no blinking this morning, Commander Sacrette." The voice of Major Sergei Zuberov shook Sacrette's headset.

"The bastard," Sacrette breathed hatefully. "He's listening in on our crypto frequency." Pressing the microphone button, Sacrette responded, telling the Soviet pilot, "Major Zuberov, this is Commander Sacrette, USS *Valiant*. Please state your intentions."

"Our intention is to prevent the vessel from farther encroachment into our perimeter."

"By what methods?" Sacrette didn't want to hear what he already suspected was the answer.

"By whatever methods are necessary."

"You son of a bitch. I've seen your methods before." He was speaking to Zuberov, who was now dead center in his gunsight display.

One of the unique features of the F-18 is the HOTAS, the hands-on throttle and stick. It allows the pilot to utilize every system in the fighter with one hand.

With his free hand, Sacrette signaled the Russian a personal message with his middle finger.

"Very amusing, Commander. May I ask your intentions?" Zuberov's voice was calm.

Playing the multitude of buttons and switches on the HOTAS like a piccolo, Sacrette armed the M61 20mm cannon mounted forward of the cockpit, increased power, and bat-turned, flying outbound to set up a gun-run.

The distance was too close for missiles; the AIM-7 Sparrow missiles stationed on the pylons beneath the wings couldn't be used safely within a half mile.

Guns were his weapon of choice; the choice of most fighter pilots. It made the combat more personal. "My intentions, Major Zuberov, are to blow your asses out of the sky if your helos don't stand off station. Immediately."

Sacrette turned on the gun-run. The lead Hind flown by Zuberov appeared like a giant dragonfly in the hazy morning air. On his flanks, the remaining Hinds danced lazily, Their missiles useless against the fighter. But Sacrette knew the doorgunners and the four-barreled 20mm cannons in the nose turrents could lay down a carpet of deadly, withering fire.

"I'm ordering you off station, Major. You're not killing these children. Take your brats home. Now!" His finger began to close around the trigger.

At the precious split millisecond before both Sacrette and Zuberov would have fired simultaneously, the voice of Captain Lord brought the play to an abrupt halt.

"Commander Sacrette. Hold fire. Repeat. Hold your fire . . . and depart your station. Repeat. Withdraw from station. Red Cell leader, return to base. Do you copy!"

Sacrette felt the gushing pace of his flowing adrenaline suddenly stem.

In his gut, a slow, aching burn gnawed painfully. Slowly, his finger moved away from the trigger.

"Perhaps another time, Commander." Zuberov's chiding voice added to Boulton Sacrette's growing rage.

Sacrette shoved the power into Zone Five, igniting the afterburner. Riding on a tongue of flame, he shot straight for the Soviet gunships, passing overhead only feet from the turning rotors of Zuberov's Hind.

"Eat that," was all he could think of saying to the Russian.

Peeling off to the west, Sacrette stayed low, his head constantly looking back until the hair-tingling suggestion creeping along his spine burst into stunning reality.

A single streak shot from the starboard stub wing of the lead Hind.

A long, white trail marked the AT-6's track.

Two seconds later, the *World Friendship* vaporized.

28

1215.

THE STORM HAD PASSED, LEAVING IN ITS WAKE A rolling, pitching sea; a sea still determined to withhold its dead.

The sky above the *Friendship*'s point of loss throbbed with the pulsation of helicopter blades. On the surface, the USS *Valiant* turned a slow rotation around the POL, her deck filled with sailors scanning for any sign of life.

The full contingency of Battle Group Zulu Station was thrown into the rescue and recovery effort of the *World Friendship*. After five hours, the results were little more than nothing.

"Do you see anything?" Sacrette yelled to Slattery over the roar of the Sea Stallion.

"Nothing human. Dead or alive. All I see is floating debris." Slattery pointed to an object floating one hundred feet beneath the opened door of the Stallion. "Looks like a mast."

Sacrette scanned the charred remains of the *World Friendship*'s mainmast with his binoculars. Motioning to the pilot, he ordered, "Take her down."

The Sea Stallion dropped to a stationary hover five feet off the surface. Sacrette knelt, staring at the main-

---

mast, which was nearly intact. Pointing at the base, where one of the yellow barrels had been positioned at the step of the mast, Sacrette noted aloud, "She snapped clean from her deck step."

Looking at the one-hundred-foot mast, he shook his head at the magnitude required to cause such destruction. "God almighty, Deke. They never had a chance."

"There was no one on deck. None that I could see, at least. They must have all been belowdecks. That's why we can't find any bodies." He shrugged. "I suppose the terrs thought the Russians wouldn't call their bluff."

Sacrette shook his head slowly. He seemed to be trying to imagine the hellacious fear sweeping the children at the moment the missile struck, igniting over four thousand pounds of Chezh Symtex.

Although it was difficult to understand the result, the total destruction, what was more difficult to understand had haunted Sacrette since the vessel was first reported approaching the Soviet perimeter.

"Why, Deke? Why did they push it so close to the edge? There was no reason. It simply doesn't make sense."

Slattery took a deep breath; releasing it slowly, he offered his only answer. "Mistake in judgment. Poor navigation. Poor seamanship. It could have been a multitude of things, Boulton."

That wasn't good enough for Sacrette. "No. Those bastards were pulling it off beautifully. Not a single goddamned mistake in three days. Navigation. Seamanship. All perfect. Even the breaks were coming their way."

"Three days with little or no sleep. Three days under the eye of the world. That's a lot of pressure. Pressure that can create mistakes."

Sacrette started to order the pilot to lift off when

something curious caught his eye. Pulling off his flight boots, then his flight suit without explanation, he stepped through the door, hitting the water moments later.

Slattery wore a look of sheer astonishment. Shouting to Sacrette, he asked, "What in the hell are you doing?"

Sacrette said nothing. Instead, he swam to the mainmast. Starting at the step, he worked his way along the full length, pausing occasionally to examine the structure.

Nearing the end, where the mainmast tapered, he recognized something peculiar. The yardarm from the main skysail was still connected to the mainmast, though dangling loose just below the surface.

Hoisting the yardarm from the water, he balanced the heavy cross-spar on the mast, then closely examined the uppermost yard of the *World Friendship*.

Running his hand along the charred wood, he suddenly paused, then looked up at Slattery, who was kneeling in the door.

The propwash whipped up a skirt of water around the base of the helo, but not enough to prevent Slattery from viewing Sacrette through the curtain separating the fighter pilot from the commando.

Sacrette wore a grin that stretched from ear to ear.

"Come here," Sacrette shouted.

Slattery dropped into the water beside Sacrette. Reaching for the SEAL's neck, Sacrette tapped the wire saw dangling like a necklace around Slattery's neck.

"Give me your saw," was all he said.

Not understanding, but complying out of curiosity, Slattery removed the wire saw from around his neck.

After five minutes, Sacrette had separated the yardarm from the mainmast. Both were helped into the helo by a crewman, then sat on the deck, staring at the yard-arm.

Slattery, still confused, asked, "What do we do with this thing, Thunderbolt?"

"Evidence," Sacrette replied bluntly.

"What evidence?" Slattery was still confused.

Sacrette wiped at the salt residue stinging his eyes; a knowing smile suddenly appeared. "Evidence that Mohammad Abu Jemal is one sly son of a bitch!"

"I don't follow you, Boulton."

Boulton sat back, resting against the bulkhead. The face of Elaine Winters appeared. Her mouth moved. Nothing. Her mouth moved again. The words became a whisper. Again she spoke.

Sacrette heard her shout until his ears rang with the woman's dying words.

Sacrette looked at Slattery. "I know why we can't find any of the bodies."

29

"SEA RESCUE REPORTS THEY HAVE NOT FOUND A single body." Captain Lord was in the CIC, talking on the red telephone. He released the button near the mouthpiece, allowing his words to scramble en route to the admiral on the Pentagon end of the line.

"No, sir," he answered when asked again. "Not a single body. My official report will conclude that the terrorists—and the children—must have all gone down with the ship."

After completing his report, Lord hung up and walked to the captain's chair on the bridge.

He looked haggard, worn through by the defeat. Gone was the exhilaration, the anticipation, the adrenaline-pumping feeling he had felt in waking to the mission. Elation was replaced by emptiness.

The emptiness was bad enough; the failure intolerable. "We didn't even get into the game."

He was speaking to the vastness of the flight deck, where the final remnants of Operation Valiant Rapier were disappearing belowdeck.

The assault helicopter wing had removed its helos from staging on the port catapult.

Two F-18s sat at Alert Five, standard procedure.

Deck crews, who had been waiting impatiently for the word on the mission status, had withdrawn to the bowels of the carrier.

A fortune had been spent in the preparation; hundreds of thousands of dollars. Not to mention the human waste. Children.

The heavy sadness suddenly became overwhelming and for the first time since graduating from the Naval Academy, he began questioning his purpose.

Standing, he started from the bridge, figuring the solitude of his sea cabin would be more medicinal than the flight deck, which was a stinging reminder of failure.

As he walked out of the bridge, his thoughts drifted to the Soviet battle group commander. He knew Admiral Sholton. He was tough, but a good man. One of the few Soviet officers with the courage to criticize Soviet intervention in Afghanistan during the Brezhnev leadership.

By any other name, the *Friendship* presented the same threat as a "fire ship" during the early days of naval warfare. A ship laden with explosives, sailing through other ships. A threat to the integrity of the battle group.

A threat no captain would tolerate. Sholton had had no other choice. Given the same circumstances, Lord would have made the same decision.

That was his only consolation at the moment. He didn't have to give the order. However, he was responsible for recovering the bodies. A task that seemed to add itself to the growing list of failures suffered by Valiant Rapier.

Inside his sea cabin, Lord had no more than dropped onto his bunk when a knock on his door brought him to his feet.

Sacrette and Slattery were standing in the corridor.

"Captain Lord," Sacrette began. "We would like you to come to the ready room."

Lord half expected to see Sacrette wearing the same look of defeat; instead, there was something devious in the way he stood, his hands propped on his hips.

"For what purpose?"

Slattery stood behind Sacrette; he was holding the yardarm recovered from the *Friendship*'s mainmast. "Boulton's playing another one of his hunches. It's a long shot. But I think you ought to hear him out. We'll need to assemble in the ready room."

Lord nodded. "I'll join you in five minutes."

Sacrette and Slattery strutted down the hall; the SEAL commander carried the yardarm on his shoulder as though it were a baseball bat.

30

PASSING THROUGH THE BULKHEAD DOOR OF THE ready room, Captain Lord found Sacrette and Slattery standing at one of the television sets near the podium.

The screen was on; a young ensign stood with his nose nearly touching the screen. He was holding a magnifying glass to the image of the *World Friendship*, which sat frozen on the screen.

"What's this all about, Commander?"

"Give us a couple of minutes, Captain," Sacrette replied. Turning back to the ensign, whom Lord recognized as the ship's photo analysis expert, Sacrette nodded for him to continue.

Ensign Charles Hyde leaned into the screen. With the magnifying glass he examined the still photo of the *Friendship*. Lord recognized the photo. The image was gray, taken earlier that morning by the *LaCrosse* satellite, whose infrared capability included cloud penetration.

"Is this what you mean, Commander?" Hyde was pointing to the *Friendship*'s stern.

Sacrette stepped closer. He smiled. "Yes. That's the baby. Now, advance the tape to the point prior to the explosion."

Hyde pressed the advance button on the VCR remote control unit, running the tape forward.

Lord saw the ship dance wildly as the tape speeded up to the point where the *Friendship* vaporized.

"Hold it right there." Sacrette's voice grew excited. "Now. Run her back to the moment just before the explosion."

The ensign complied. In slow motion, the exploding ship began to rematerialize.

A bright orange fireball dissolved into the sea; masts and upper decks were suddenly reunited. In seconds, the ship was pitching on the surface, her bow plowing through the stormy surface.

"Stop!" Sacrette ordered. The screen snapped to an abrupt halt. The *Friendship* sat frozen only moments before disintegration.

"Take a look now, Ensign. I'll bet you a thousand dollars our little gray shadow is gone."

Hyde leaned again to the screen. He put the magnifying glass directly over the *Friendship*'s stern. Seconds passed, then Hyde spoke softly, telling Sacrette, "You're right, Commander!"

Slattery clapped his hands together loudly. "Good man, Boulton. Damn good man."

His patience worn thin, Lord growled, "Would you gentlemen tell me what in the Sam-Hell you're doing?"

Sacrette leaned against the podium. Jerking his head to the screen, he said, "Look at that photo, Captain. Just aft of the helm. Near the stern. What do you see?"

Lord took the magnifying glass. He saw nothing except the empty deck of a ship destined for eternity. "I don't see anything of special significance."

Sacrette grinned. He nodded to Hyde. "Run her back to the photo taken at oh-four-hundred."

"While he's obeying your order, Commander, per-

haps you'll obey mine and tell me what you're up to."
Lord's face didn't share the comical enthusiasm of his
subordinates.

Slattery held up the yardarm. "It started with this
yardarm, Captain. Boulton retrieved it from the water.
It's the yardarm to the mainmast. Specifically, it's the
main skysail yard."

"Meaning what, Major?"

"Meaning . . ." Sacrette interrupted. He took the
yardarm. "This." He ran his hand along the yard.

Lord stared for a moment at the yardarm. The wood
was charred slightly, but in fairly good condition considering what it had gone through. He examined it closely,
allowing his eyes to cover every visible inch. Finally, he
swallowed, and for the first time since seeing the *Friendship* disintegrate, he allowed himself a slight smile. "I'll
be damned."

"Yes, sir," Sacrette added. He ran his hand along
the yardarm. "Something missing, Captain?"

Lord nodded excitedly. "There certainly is something missing. The *Friendship* was an exact replica of an
early twentieth century windjammer. The buntlines
were made of wire rope for hoisting the sails."

Sacrette ran his hand along the yardarm. "No buntlines. They've been cut. Even with that enormous explosion there would have been something left of the sail
and rigging. But there's nothing. She's been stripped
clean."

"What are you suggesting?"

Sacrette looked at the *Friendship* , which Hyde now
had projecting from the four o'clock morning surveillance. "When the *Friendship* exploded, her masts were
clean. In close examination of the ship prior to explosion,
there were no furlings on the yardarms."

"You mean all the sails were stripped from the masts?"

"That's exactly what I mean."

"For what purpose?"

Sacrette shrugged. "The obvious. Expediency. The terrs would have needed at least an hour or two to lower the sails. In that storm, it would have been a near-impossible task. Therefore, they simply climbed the rigging, then cut the sails, letting them fall to the sea. They probably used wire-cutters. Snip. Snip. Buntlines. Lift tackle. All the rigging."

"Why?"

Again the Sacrette grin flashed. "So the ship could run on auxiliary power. Her course guided by automatic pilot."

Lord shook his head. "I still don't understand."

Sacrette pointed to the television screen. "Now. Look at this photo of the ship. It was taken at zero-four-hundred. Look very carefully at the stern. Just aft of the helm. Tell me what you see?"

Lord took the magnifying glass. He examined the stern. "There's something lying on the deck." He looked again, beginning to feel something familiar about the shape of the object resting on the dead ship's deck.

Sacrette pointed at Slattery. "It was Deke who figured it out."

Slattery put his finger next to the dark object. "That is a zodiac rubber boat."

Sacrette piped in, adding, "A zodiac rubber boat used by the terrs to abandon ship after they stripped the rigging, then sent the ship on autopilot toward the Soviet perimeter. An act they knew would provoke the Russians."

"The murderous bastards!" Lord's voice was filled

with loathing. "They stripped the ship, aimed her toward the Soviets, then left those children to be murdered."

Sacrette and Slattery started laughing. Lord wasn't amused by their macabre behavior, and was prompted to ask, "What do you find so damn funny about the ruthless slaughter of innocent children?"

Sacrette shook his head. Before the CAG could respond, Lord was overwhelmed by the sudden realization.

"My God! There were no children aboard the ship. They're still alive. Along with the terrorists!"

31

1538.

KAHLIL SALAMAN COULD FEEL HER EYES; HE COULD feel her hatred. She said nothing but her silence spoke with a loathing more definitive than words. Loathing that cuts to the deepest quick. Loathing that sends the most profound message.

Finally he spoke, posing the question directly. "You are Israeli?"

Ilyannha sat against the cold, dank wall of the hull. Having grown immune to the smell, an inconvenience she had disciplined herself to ignore since the hijacking, she applied the same discipline to her captor.

Kahlil rose, acting as though he was stretching his legs while casually inching his way toward the rows of bunks where Ilyannha sat watching his approach. Carefully, he threaded his way through a maze of mattresses spread on the floor; pausing, he examined the faces and, when satisfied that the children were sleeping, continued his approach.

Drawing her legs up, she coiled her body, ready to spring when he stepped into her range. Sensing that he must realize she was waiting, she relaxed as Kahlil, who appeared as nothing more than a shadow among shadows, paused just beyond her range.

"I asked a question. Are you Israeli?"

"I am French," she replied.

She could see his head move from side to side; his words confirmed his doubt. "No. You are Israeli."

Ilyannha threw back her head. "Why is that important?"

"We know there are three Israelis in your group. Identify the remaining two . . . it will be better for the others."

"What makes you think I'm Israeli?"

Kahlil detected genuine curiosity in her voice. "You are not afraid."

Ilyannha laughed sarcastically. "Of course I'm afraid."

"No," he snapped. "I know fear. I know Israelis. Israelis do not fear Palestinians. You think we are less than human."

"You are a terrorist. That is less than human."

"I'm not a terrorist. I am fedayeen. Ashbal. A soldier of Palestine."

Again she laughed. "You are nothing but children." She pointed to the dark shapes lying on the mattresses. "Like all of us. The only difference . . . you have guns."

"Yes. We have guns. In Gaza . . . we had only rocks for weapons." His hand touched the stone hanging around his neck.

"Gaza? Is that what this is all about?"

"You have heard about what is happening in Gaza?"

"The whole world has heard. It's no secret."

He shook his head. "People have seen what the Israelis allow them to see. They have seen the *intifadeh* . . . the riots . . . the soldiers. They have seen everything but the truth."

"The truth?" Ilyannha found this statement curious. "What truth?"

"What we are fighting for."

"What are you fighting for? A Palestinian state? Israel will never agree to a Palestinian state within the territorial boundaries of Israel."

Kahlil shook his head vigorously. "They are trying to destroy the children! Destroy the Palestinian children . . . the Israelis eliminate the problem in the future."

Ilyannha couldn't believe her ears. "Destroy the children! That's absurd."

Kahlil's hand slapped emphatically against the metallic receiver of his AK-47. "No. It's not absurd. It's the truth. The older ones . . . our brothers and sisters . . . have all been destroyed. The PLO. Fateh. The Popular Front. All destroyed. Spread to the corners of the earth like ashes on the wind. Now, the Israelis are turning to Gaza, to the last of the Palestinians. Where there is *intifadeh*—rebellion. The government justifies the destruction of Gaza in the name of civil obedience. Schools have been closed. Palestinian children are not being educated, creating a future generation of illiteracy. Businesses destroyed—Arab businesses! What are the Arab businessmen to do? The Israelis have taken over their businesses. They live in the streets like beggars, or must move to another country. It is the new Israeli policy."

Ilyannha snapped to her feet. "No. It is not the policy of Israel. The Israeli soldiers despise what's going on in Gaza. They detest having to face children, which, I might add, lends to the cowardliness of the Palestinian people. Using children, the most vile of all methods. What you have lost in war you try to regain through world opinion, destroying the most precious of your resources—your children. You!"

Kahlil's eyes turned to flame. His hand swept outward, clipping Ilyannha behind the knees.

Crashing to the deck, she felt him move swiftly astride her.

She could taste his breath; his hatred burned like a candle through the darkness of the hold. And, she realized, he was wrong: she was afraid!

Kahlil's fingers tore at her T-shirt. The softness of her skin aroused him, heightening his anger. He was sworn to the celibacy of the *mujihadeen*; his arousal seemed to overwhelm his spiritual commitments, drowning him with shame.

Shame that enhanced his fury.

"I am not a child. I am a man. I will show you I am a man!"

Ilyannha tried to fight, but his physical advantage, coupled with his sexual arousal left her defenseless. She heard crying from the children awakening on the floor. Shouts began to fill the hold. Screams rang off the slimy walls, echoing throughout the lower deck.

Pulling at her panties, Kahlil didn't hear the clanging of the bulkhead door.

He didn't see the figure moving through the darkness. He felt nothing but the fiery need to humiliate, to satisfy his own anger.

A heavy hand reached through the darkness, then pulled away, gripping Kahlil by the hair. Jerking him upright, the interloper flung the flailing boy backward.

"Are you insane!" the voice called through the darkness.

Kahlil said nothing. He dove for his weapon. The interloper's foot raced outward, pinning the AK-47 to the slippery deck. Grabbed by the scruff of the neck, Kahlil felt himself being towed helplessly. A strong shaft of light appeared as the door opened. In the next instant, the young Ashbal soared through the door, where he crashed in a heap in the dimly lit hall outside the hold.

Ilyannha recoiled at the ringing of the closing door. The hold was silent, the children quiet. Wondering. Waiting. She felt the presence of the man, but through the darkness she saw nothing.

Suddenly a deep, heavily accented voice broke the silence. "You should not provoke the boy. He is very dangerous."

Ilyannha slipped farther back onto the bunk. She tried to cover her breasts, but the T-shirt was shredded. Reaching over the side, she groped for several seconds, finally recovering her shorts. She quickly dressed, then shrank again into the thick blackness of the bunk.

"I didn't provoke him," Ilyannha finally said, trying to determine where the man was standing.

"You must have. He is a highly disciplined young man. He does not lose his temper so easily."

After a long silence, she said, "Thank you."

The stranger grumped as a long tongue of fire skipped through the veil of blackness.

Ilyannha sat forward, catching a momentary glimpse of the man who had saved her from Kahlil. She saw a thick beard framing a weathered face; his eyes appeared blacker than the darkness.

He touched a flame to his pipe, sucked in heavily, venting plumes of smoke that appeared copper against the fire from the match. Momentarily, the match flickered, then died, returning the hold to a velvety darkness.

"Who are you?" she asked.

From the blackness, the deep voice replied, "Raspides. The captain of this ship."

32

"IT WAS WHAT THE CHAPERONE WAS TRYING TO TELL me. It was why she was shot by Jemal. They took the ship, then transported the children to another vessel. They used her and the *Friendship* as a red herring while the children were being moved out of the area. They must have anticipated that we would have to try a rescue mission once the Israelis put the kabosch on their demands."

Lord listened to Sacrette; it began to make sense. "Of course. Once the Israeli government rejected the demands, Israel would be held responsible for the outcome."

Slattery added his observation. "With the children presumed dead, the manure would really hit the Israeli westinghouse. I would bet the Israeli government is dodging more international flak since invading Lebanon."

"Precisely. World opinion that will become even greater." Lord was looking at the *Friendship*, feeling foolish at having been outfoxed.

Sacrette whistled. "Man. When the world learns those children are alive, that they've been brought back from the grave, every country on this planet will be breathing down the Israelis' neck to give in to the terrorists."

"That was what they were planning on." Lord suddenly seemed revived. "Which means we've got work to do." He thought for a moment. Finally, he told Sacrette, "Commander, we have to find that ship carrying the children."

"I know."

"Any suggestions of where we start?"

Sacrette walked in a circle, allowing his thoughts to roam. Pausing to reexamine the screen depicting the *Friendship*, his mind began tumbling backward, replaying the events of the past three days.

Finally, like a landslide playing out its energy, his brain came to a halt on an obscure item included in Captain Lord's initial briefing of the hijacking. "In the first briefing, you mentioned that a ship had been contacted by the terrorists."

Without speaking, Lord reached into his briefcase. Removing a file marked TOP SECRET above the words *Operation Valiant Rapier*, he began turning through pages until he reached the bottom page, a transcript of the initial coded conversation with the Pentagon. "The Pentagon reported a freighter under Greek registry was contacted by the terrorists."

"The freighter's name?"

"The *Helenas*."

Sacrette pointed at the folder. "Does it give the freighter's last port of call?"

Lord shook his head. "No. But that can be determined easily enough. I'll contact the Greek government. The Maritime Ministry will have the information on record."

A knowledgeable smirk inched across Sacrette's

face. "I can tell you the *Helenas*'s last port of call."

"How?"

Pointing at one of the yellow barrels on the deck of the *Friendship*, Sacrette said, "Bulgaria. Sophia, more than likely."

"What makes you say that?"

Sacrette shrugged. "That's where the Chezh Symtex was reported stolen by the CIA!"

33

1700.

SACRETTE HAD PLAYED A HUNCH; A HUNCH THAT
answered many of the mysteries surrounding the fate of
the hijacked children. Still, final confirmation was
needed by the Pentagon and other forces involved in the
situation. More importantly for Sacrette, there was his
compelling need to know the truth.

"Home Plate . . . this is Wolf One, reporting at Angel's twelve." Sacrette released the microphone switch
on the HOTAS, waiting for the response.

In the distance, a solitary black speck was visible
on the surface. In the background, the loam-colored coast
of Libya lay less than forty nautical miles away.

Sacrette figured the terrorists used the storm, and
the proximity of the Soviet perimeter to provide con-
fusion and cover to make their escape. The *Helenas,* no
doubt cruising in the area, would have gone unnoticed.
The sea was open to traffic of all nations.

"Smart move," he said aloud, thinking of the courage it must have taken to make such a bold move. He
glanced at the black dot, which was now larger, taking
on the shape of a freighter. "You slipped in, picked up
the terrs, then beat a course for Libya. You left the world
thinking the children died aboard the *World Friendship.*

That would give you plenty of time to make an end run to Qaddafiland. Question is: What are you going to do next?"

Before he could consider the thought, Captain Lord's voice resounded in the cockpit of the F-18 Hornet, ordering, "Umpire to Wolf One. You are cleared for visual. Maintain surprise, and observation. You are now in unfriendly territory."

Gripping the HOTAS, Sacrette pushed the nose forward, kicked left rudder and left aileron, putting the fighter into a steep spiral.

The ocean began revolving around the nose of the *Crunch 'n' Munch* as Sacrette's fighter screamed from the sky. Directly ninety degrees from his angle of attack, Sacrette saw the horizon gradually slide up and away from his line of sight. The only color was the blue of the sea; and the brilliant sunlight splashing off his instrument panel, partially obscuring the red digital readout on the HUD, which swam in golden sunlight.

Two hundred feet above the deck, Sacrette eased back on the HOTAS, bringing the nose to level flight.

Glancing to the west, he saw the sun; a quick calculation, followed by a heading change of seventy degrees, and he was ready.

Lowering the nose, Sacrette shoved the throttle through military power, into Zone Five.

The sky quaked as the twin afterburners launched the F-18 on its new course.

34

JEMAL STOOD ON THE FORECASTLE, THE SPACE BE-
neath the short raised forward deck of the *Helenas*. Below,
on the main deck, the Ashbal were finishing their prayers.
He wore a sullen look; the acidity of fatigue evident.

A quick check of his watch prompted Jemal to raise
his binoculars. Tuning the focus, he saw a clear, placid
surface.

In the background, he saw the loam-colored cliffs
of Tobruk, which brought a pleased look to his face.

"It is very beautiful, the North African coast."

Jemal turned to Raspides, who now approached,
wiping his oil-slick fingers with a rag.

"What about the engines?" Jemal asked, not caring
about the beauty. "Are they working?"

Raspides turned his hands up in uncertainty. "For
the moment. That's not to say they will not quit again.
The storm was more punishment than anticipated." He
looked at Jemal, noting that the terrorist had lost weight
in the past three days. "You should eat, *fendi*. You look
like a sick tree."

The thought of food sent a painful, sickening ripple
through Jemal's stomach; a stomach now longing for the
steadiness of land.

"I will eat in Tobruk."

Raspides pointed at the Libyan coast. "Yes. Tobruk. Where our arrangement finally ends. Thank God."

"Praise be to Allah. I will be rid of you and your stinking ship forever."

Raspides hawked and spit. "What are your plans once you reach Tobruk?"

Jemal shook his head. "That is none of your concern."

Raspides didn't appear insulted. "I was merely curious."

"Curious!" Jemal laughed. "You would sell the information to the Americans. Perhaps to your government to save your own skin. You are a man without principles, Raspides. A mercenary who would sell his own mother for the right price."

Raspides didn't take offense; he was never bothered by the truth. "I understand you won't be taking the children to the desert?"

Jemal turned slightly. He was looking at the sea merchant's bearded throat. The statement had come as a surprise. Bringing with it a warning that immediately put Jemal on the defensive. A warning that coincided with what was now appearing on the southern horizon, where the blue sea joined the loam-colored outline of the Libyan coast. "You ask too many questions," was all he said.

What he was thinking was altogether different.

Jemal turned quickly. Leaning over the rail, he shouted to the main deck, "Kahlil!" He motioned for the boy.

Running up the steps leading to the forecastle, Jemal carried an AK–47 at port arms. He was wearing camouflaged fatigues beneath a webbed harness. Grenades hung from the harness, along with three pouches of loaded AK-47 magazines.

Jemal whispered to Kahlil; a look of hesitance and surprise suddenly clouded the boy's features.

Appearing reluctant, Jemal pointed to the main deck. "Do as you're told," Jemal's angry voice ordered.

Kahlil nodded obediently, then hurried down the steps to the other Ashbal. He spoke to them hurriedly; momentarily, they dashed away, disappearing through several bulkheads leading to other parts of the ship.

Raspides paid no attention to their comings and goings; he seemed lost to the beauty of the sea. In his mind, he was spending the money he would be paid for transporting the terrorists to Tobruk. After Tobruk, he would confront the allegations he had anticipated before he agreed to join Jemal.

Allegations that could be easily explained. His ship had been hijacked by the terrorists. Forced to take them to Tobruk, he could do nothing against their overwhelming firepower.

He was the captain of the *Helenas*. His ship and crew came first, above all other considerations. Even terrorism.

He felt Jemal shifting his stance at his side. A smile moved his bearded face. A smile that suddenly froze at the razor sting beneath his ribcage. At the hot, searing wave rushing through his body, rendering his legs nearly useless.

"You know too much, óld man." Jemal's hot breath burned in Raspides's ear.

Looking down at Jemal's muscled arm, Raspides's terror-stricken eyes slowly took in the Arab's hand, which was pressed hard against his ribcage.

Jemal's hand turned a bloodstained dagger, sending

another wave of nausea and pain jolting through the captain's upper body.

Shoving his knee beneath Raspides's buttocks, Jemal supported the captain's dying weight. Glancing quickly to the bridge, he saw Kahlil and Layla enter, their weapons pointed at the first mate steering the ship.

Shouts began to fill the calm air above the *Helenas* as the Ashbal appeared on deck, brandishing their weapons menacingly at the *Helenas's* crew, who walked with their arms above their heads.

Raspides tried to speak; blood filled his mouth as the dagger tore again at his lungs.

Jemal jerked his head toward the south. "Our friends have arrived. An escort. You are no longer necessary."

Raspides's dying eyes turned to the south, to the sea where he'd spent all his life.

Two white frigates raced toward the *Helenas*. Flying high above their bridges, Libyan flags bent back, swept aft by the speed.

A roar began to fill Raspides's ears; a distant, pulsating roar. He began to slide down Jemal's leg; his fingers gripped at the rail, but the strength to hold himself upright was gone.

The roar grew, like a freight train running out of control, and knowing there was no railroad on the open sea, Raspides looked one last time at the sky.

In his last moment of life, he recognized the bright red tongue of fire appearing from out of the flaming sun.

35

"I SEE THE LITTLE BASTARDS!" SACRETTE SPOKE calmly into his mouthpiece. In the instant that his F-18 flashed across the bow of the *Helenas*, he caught sight of the Ashbal on the main deck.

"These boys like taking things that don't belong to them. If I'm not mistaken...they're hijacking the freighter!" Sacrette added, suddenly realizing what was happening.

"What do you see, Wolf One?" the umpire requested.

Sacrette wasn't listening. His eyes were fixed on the frigates approaching from the south.

"Well, well," he said with a smile. "Look who's coming for dinner."

"What is the situation, Wolf One?" The Umpire's voice sounded impatient.

"We've got Lib bathtubs, Home Plate. Two Susa-class frigates. They appear to be homing in on the *Helenas*."

The Umpire paused, then asked, "Are their intentions hostile?"

"I'll ask them!" Sacrette's F-18 shot past the frigates, sending geysers of water spewing skyward as the afterburner exhaust exploded off the surface.

Two seconds later, Sacrette's cockpit filled with the warning shriek of heat lock-on.

The radar scope came alive as three heat-seeking missiles streaked from the surface.

"They're pissed off, Umpire. I'm locked up with three gomers! Going to flares and evasive!"

Sacrette unloaded a string of flares from the chaff/flair dispenser, sprinkling the sky with a golden stream of heat-producing flares, then pulled back on the HOTAS, sending the F-18 into a pure vertical climb.

Through the g-force pummeling his senses, his eyes watched the radar scope, where one of the blips suddenly disappeared.

"One down . . . two to go," Sacrette spoke to himself as he rolled inverted, picking up the two approaching missiles on his radar screen.

The F-18 dove straight for the sea at Mach 1.8, shoving Thunderbolt into his seat with such force that he could only watch the radar scope as the missiles picked up his heat signature, then pursued in trail.

Calmly, he pressed the chaff/flare release button, dispensing another string of parachute flares from near the port main gear well.

Another blip disappeared from the radar scope.

"Two down . . . and one to take downtown." A wicked grin crinkled his brow as he pulled back on the HOTAS with all his strength.

The last missile was closing.

Sacrette lined up on the lead Libyan frigate. "You boys need a lesson in manners. Fox Two," he said softly, the signal indicating launch of a Sidewinder missile.

Locked onto the frigate, Sacrette launched an AIM-9L Sidewinder missile from his starboard wingtip, then pulled back on the HOTAS and shoved the throttles through Zone Five, riding the afterburner surge while turning his eyes to the radar screen.

The Libyan missile, unable to turn as quickly, picked up on the heat source of the Sidewinder.

From the bow of the freighter, Jemal watched as the American fighter, who had seemed destined to crash in the sea only moments before, had fired one missile, then raced for the heavens.

In his next heartbeat, Jemal watched the American missile strike the Libyan frigate, followed by the Libyan missile, which struck the deck only feet from where its deadly journey began.

A thunderous explosion rocked the surface, sending shockwaves toward the freighter. An orange-gray ball of flame could be seen licking the sky where the frigate had cruised only moments before. Then, near the curtain of water cascading down from where the frigate exploded, the second frigate appeared miraculously.

Jemal's heart lifted from the despair at seeing the first frigate explode. "Kill him! Kill the American!" Jemal shouted.

As though hearing the threat directed at his aircraft, Sacrette replied softly, "Eat my shorts!" His hand gripped the firing mechanism. He had the frigate locked into his sights, and knew the signal was now transmitting lock-on to the Libyan command center.

The thought of the Libyans, who would be frantic by now, sent a thrill racing along Sacrette's spine.

On the bow, Jemal's heart fell as he saw the Libyan frigate turn to port, execute a rapid one-eighty, and scurry for the sanctuary of their twelve-mile border, which lay in the near distance.

Realizing the *Helenas* could be the next target, Jemal

shouted to Kahlil. "Bring the children on deck. Hurry. There isn't much time."

Still maintaining lock-on to the frigate, Sacrette rolled in from the north, set up an attack angle, then pressed the firing mechanism. "Fox Two," he reported to the *Valiant* CIC.

Seconds later, the sea shook, reverberating as the missile struck with its twenty-two pounds of deadly HE explosives.

Sacrette saw the bridge explode, then noticed the crew jumping over the sides. A black plume of smoke began to rise gloriously into the sky, marking the frigate's damaged struggle toward Libya.

"What's the situation, Wolf One?" The excited voice of Captain Lord rang in Sacrette's ears.

Sacrette grinned, then replied, "One Lib frigate sunk; the second on fire and returning to port."

Lord spoke against the background noise enveloping the CIC, where the cheering drowned anything he might have said. When the cheers subsided, Lord asked, "What about the *Helenas*? Do you see anything?"

Taking a quick glance, Sacrette saw the main deck fill with a variety of people. Figures with camouflage fatigues, carrying weapons, encircled other figures. He noticed that the figures inside the circle were wearing white T-shirts.

"I see a group of approximately two dozen people wearing white T-shirts."

Lord's voice came back excitedly. "Return to Home Plate, Wolf One. You've found the children."

DAY FOUR

36

0130. Battle Group Zulu Station. Off the coast of Libya.

CAPTAIN ELROD LORD'S FACE SWAM IN A SEA OF SOFT red light flooding the CIC. Leaning against a bulkhead, he spoke in a low voice on the red telephone.

The dejection on his features shone with painful clarity; never had he felt so close to despair.

The sigh of relief that had swept the Western world with the discovery that the hostage children were alive had dissipated with the speed of the sun burning away a thin carpet of morning fog. Relief had quickly given way to frustration.

The hostage children were now inside Libya, and neither Lord nor the CIA knew their location. He was beginning to feel like a one-legged man in an ass-kicking contest.

"I understand your suggestion, Mr. Zacharopolis. What you're suggesting is a long shot at best. A risky long shot. I'll explore the potential, then get back to you." Lord scrawled down a name given him by the CIA station chief from the American embassy in Athens.

Hanging up the telephone, Lord went to the bridge. Looking out over the sea, he could see a necklace of lights highlighting Tobruk against the darkness of the desert night.

"A real risky long shot," he repeated softly. Then he walked off the bridge, knowing there remained only one chance to find the children.

37

CAPTAIN LORD FOUND BOULTON SACRETTE IN THE ready room, where the CAG sat talking with Deke Slattery. The two men appeared haggard; neither had slept more than six hours during the past two days. Captain Lord had slept even less.

"Gentlemen," Lord greeted the pair with a heavy sigh.

Sacrette was sitting in his leather chair, one leg thrown over the arm. Slattery sat in the aisle; spread around him were a variety of maps, intelligence photographs from the *LaCrosse* satellite, and an old copy of *National Geographic*.

The copy of *National Geographic* was opened to a detailed story focused on the people of Libya.

Slattery took a photograph defining the vastness of Tobruk, a city cramped with copper-white houses, twisting narrow streets, buildings manufactured from sandstone. Examining the photo with a magnifying glass, he found nothing helpful, as had been the case with the other photographs.

"What have you heard from the CIA?" Slattery asked, sipping a cup of coffee.

Lord squatted above the photographs; running his

fingers over the glossy depiction of a mosque sitting on a high hill overlooking Tobruk, he added little to what they already knew.

"The CIA's Athens station chief reports his contacts have turned up nothing since the *Helenas* docked yesterday evening."

Sacrette picked up one of the photographs, gave it a sideways glance, and, finding nothing revealing, dropped the photograph onto the carpeted deck. "It doesn't make any sense. God dammit! They couldn't have vanished into thin air, Captain. Not a group that size."

Slattery tapped a photograph. Taken from twenty miles above the Libyan desert, the photo captured a small camp spread around a blue oasis. "They're still in the city. Satellite reconnaissance has maintained constant surveillance on the only Palestinian terrorist camp in the Libyan desert. Nothing has come in. Nothing has gone out."

"That's my point," Sacrette said. "If they're still in the city . . . somebody must have seen something. You can't just hide twenty-four kids without catching someone's attention."

Lord stretched his arms outward, forming his hands into two fists. Rolling his head from side to side, he felt the muscles in his neck untighten, relieving only slightly the tension that had wound his neck muscles into hardened bands. Taking a folded piece of paper from his pocket, he reread the name given him by the CIA station chief.

"Let's reexamine the facts, gentlemen. Visual contact was lost shortly after the freighter docked. CIA reports the children were put aboard a bus, then transported through the city to the bazaar. That's where we lost them."

"Shrewd," Slattery commented. "They knew we would be tracking them by satellite. So they melted into the crowd, and now they could be in a thousand different places."

"Just like Beirut," Sacrette added.

"Worse," replied Lord, staring coldly at the piece of paper. "If it were Beirut we'd have some means of intelligence gathering. Tobruk is the coldest burner on the Middle East stove. Intelligence on the city is sparse at best; nonexistent at worst. Matter of fact, the CIA says there's only one American resident in the entire city."

"An American? That's odd. I wouldn't think an American could live in Libya. What's his status?" asked Sacrette, appearing genuinely surprised.

"Martin Thornson. A retired air force master sergeant. He married a Moslem shortly before the Libs chased the United States out of Wheelus Air Base in Tripoli. The Libyan government permitted him to return after his retirement. It seems Thornson's wife was the niece of a high-ranking Libyan military officer. One of Qaddafi's inner circle."

Sacrette sat forward, then winked at Slattery. "An American in Tobruk. How's that for the knock of opportunity?" His voice sounded suggestive.

Slattery's eyebrows raised slightly. "Are you thinking what I'm thinking?"

Sacrette nodded very carefully. "It might be worth a try."

Realizing his suggestion was taking root, Lord looked again at the paper bearing Thornson's name. "Sergeant Thornson lives east of Tobruk, near an oil refinery. He was a heavy equipment operator in the military. A good one by the sounds of his service record. He's currently employed at the refinery."

"Heavy equipment?" Slattery was thinking aloud. "Which means he probably has a truck."

Breaking in, Sacrette added, "A truck big enough to haul a few good tourists around the city of Tobruk."

"An expatriate with a truck." Slattery smiled. Looking at Lord, he asked, "Has the mission been approved by the Pentagon?"

Lord's face was a stern mask, delivering a message Sacrette and Slattery received within seconds.

"Holy shit," Slattery whispered. He said nothing else.

Boulton Sacrette took a deep breath, then exhaled very slowly. "There's no approval."

Lord's eyes crinkled slightly, and a thin smile was pulled from the edges of his mouth. "There's no mission."

"What about shore leave, Captain?" Slattery's mind was racing ahead. "My boys are getting anxious to get their feet back on solid ground."

"Did you bring your passports?" was the captain's reply.

A deep, throaty laugh echoed from Slattery. "Hell, Captain. We don't need passports. We'll go in sterile. Live off the land. The way we were trained."

Lord appeared to have made a decision, but cautioned, "It'll be risky. If you're caught . . ." He never finished; Slattery finished for him.

"Yes, sir. I know the script by heart. 'If we're caught, the American government will disavow any knowledge of our existence.' We've been there before, Captain. That's the beauty of the Red Cell concept . . .

we put ourselves in a situation that dictates the outcome from the beginning. We either win . . . or we lose. No middle ground."

Lord clapped his hands together loudly. "Very well, Major. What will you need?"

Slattery looked at the photographs of the coast of Libya. "One very expendable helicopter."

"And," Sacrette blurted, "one very expendable helicopter pilot."

Lord turned his eyes upward, as though seeking some divine council. "You're both crazy."

Sacrette stood, telling Lord what they all knew. "Not as crazy as you, Captain."

Lord didn't need an explanation; however, he felt he owed it to himself to know with certainty just how risky their "mission" was. This wasn't the time to be deluding oneself. "How's that?"

"All they can do is kill us." Sacrette drew his hands like a gunslinger, aiming his index fingers at Captain Lord. "If this goes bad . . . Congress, the Joint Chiefs, and the president will have you swabbing the decks of an icebreaker off the Alaskan coast."

38

THE SH-53 SEAHAWK CUT THROUGH THE AIR ABOVE
the Med, five minutes outbound from the deck of the
Valiant. In the distance, Libya was more of a blur than
reality; a place that had only existed in the abstract to
the men now flying to her shores.

Inside the helo, the Red Cell team sat in webbed
seats, each man's private thoughts a mystery to the other
members of the team.

All but one.

"It's hotter than a whore's breath under this damn
dress!" Gunny cursed, pulling at the long, flowing imi-
tation Arab dress he wore over his desert camouflage fatigues.

From the cockpit of the Seahawk, Sacrette studied
the garb worn by himself and the other members of the
Red Cell team lining the wall of the helo. "Show some
respect for expediency, Gunny. Doc Holweigner's latest
design might not be fashionable in Mississippi, but in
Libya, you're a couturiere's dream."

"A couti-what?"

"Fashion designer," Doc interrupted with the clar-
ification.

Recalling Holweigner's suggestion that they use

sheets taken from the sick bay, the tough marine replied, "Fuck the fashion. I look like a damned Klansman."

"That might be . . . but you'll blend with the human landscape, Gunny." Slattery sat beside Sacrette in the copilot's seat. His face was covered with black face paint.

Gunny looked at Slattery, then at Starlight, whose face was also black. Beaming from within the shiny blackness, his two white eyes stood out like the stripes painted on a highway. "What about Starlight? He's lit up like a hoot owl. There ain't no black man in the world with white eyes!"

Starlight slipped on a pair of sunglasses and flashed a broad smile.

Slattery pulled on a night-vision mask, covering his lighter blue eyes. "Improvisation, Gunny. Improvisation."

Settling into the seat, Slattery ignored the cussing of his team XO, turning his attention to the map spread on his lap. His finger, which appeared green through the night-vision mask, followed a red line drawn from the approximate position of the *Valiant*, to Wadi-Sabeh, a desolated point located on the east, fourteen miles from Tobruk.

Where the red line ended, the word SABEH TOWER was jotted beside a rock formation rising from what photo reconnaissance determinations concluded was the only point near Tobruk offering three vital assets: isolation, cover, and proximity to a highway.

"What's our ETA?" Slattery asked Sacrette.

"Thirteen minutes to Sabeh Tower. We've been inside Libyan territory for two minutes." Glancing out the window, Sacrette could see the sporadic spray of seawater less than five feet below the helo's 167-mph track across the water. A track that was dangerous, yet necessary to avoid radar detection.

Slattery leaned against the windshield. Raising binoculars to the starlight mask, he scanned the surface to the front. "Surface is clear. No boat traffic visible."

"Our luck's running strong," Sacrette replied. "Flying this low and fast, a windsurfer could knock us from the sky."

"Nothing out there but the black of night."

"Wrong. There's more. Including twenty-four frightened children."

39

0233.

ILYANNHA LAVI SAT WITHIN A HUMAN CIRCLE; SUR-
rounding her, the hostage children from the *World
Friendship* sat cross-legged, listening to the girl. By her
own courage she had become the leader of the group.

"Help will come. When they arrive we must be
ready," she said softly while touching as many of their
hands as possible, hoping to feel a spark of resistance.

A spark she had not seen since their capture.

The room was dark; a narrow shaft of moonlight
filtered through the French sliding doors that were
boarded over, securing the only exit from the room; other
than the door, which all knew was guarded by one of
the Ashbal.

"Ready for what?" asked Brigitte. "To run?"

Using a smile to mask her intolerance for the young
French girl's ignorance, Ilyannha replied calmly, "Not
run. There is nowhere to run. We will have to help the
soldiers. We will have to help ourselves. When they come
we will all fight together as one . . . or die together as one.
There will be no middle ground."

This notion sent a trickle through the group. Some
found the notion intriguing; most were horror-struck.

"What soldiers?" asked Johann Friege, a German teenager.

"Commandos," Ilyannha replied flatly.

"How do you know there will be commandos?" asked Dereck Olafson, a tall, gangly Norwegian.

Ilyannha didn't answer; rather, she merely felt their presence for a long moment. To think that they knew nothing of these matters was incomprehensible; it was what all Israeli children learned instinctively from childhood.

She thought for a moment. There were twenty-four. Three were Israelis.

Quickly, she turned to Raanan Herzog, a twelve-year-old from Nablos. Raised in the hotbed of Palestinian hatred, the dark-eyed Sabra would understand the situation.

"Raanan, you are trained in the martial arts," she whispered. "We will break into groups of seven. You will lead one group, while working with the other groups on how to attack with feet and hands. Teach them how to fight in the dark. How to overpower an enemy."

She turned to Yitzhak Silverman, the other Israeli, an eleven-year-old boy from Tel Aviv. "You will be responsible for a group of seven. You will teach the group about weapons. Your father is a colonel in the paratroopers." She paused, fearing she may have misjudged. "You do know about weapons, don't you?"

"Yes," his voice replied from the darkened circle.

"Good," said Ilyannha. "Show them what is important. Instruct them on the weapons the terrorists are carrying. How they work."

Had there been light, Ilyannha would have seen the boy staring at her in disbelief. "How? We do not have any weapons!"

Ilyannha thumped his head with her knuckles. "Use your head. And your imagination. Draw pictures with words. Explain how the guns work. I will take the third group."

"What will you do with the groups?" asked Raanan.

"Tactics. I will teach the groups how to defend this room. Remember. The room is very large. They will not be able to see all of us when they come in. It will be our chance. Our only chance. We must be ready when the commandos arrive." Then she added a final note of caution. "But not until we hear the commandos firing. That will be the signal. Until then, we must act like frightened cowards."

"I am a frightened coward," came a voice.

Ilyannha chuckled. As did the others. It made her feel good to laugh, even in the face of such odds. Such danger.

They were all frightened. Young and frightened.

It was then that she was drawn to the shaft of moonlight. During the day before she had peered through the crack, discovering a vast expanse of Libyan desert stretching for as far as she could see.

The glass would be useful, but the window was covered with boards.

The boards!

Ilyannha snapped to a crouch; stealthily, she inched her way to the moonlight, drawn like a moth.

The doors were boarded with a wall of planking held to the floor and their frame by metal studs. As she ran her hand over the crack, a splinter stung her flesh but she ignored the biting sting. Digging her fingernails into the crack, she pried until her fingernails snapped.

The crack was wider.

Again she tried; the crack grew as the blood began to run down her fingers.

Five minutes passed; five minutes of painful coaching of the rough wood with her bleeding fingers.

Finally, a long, sharp splinter pulled away, bleeding more light into the room. Excited by the light, the children slid and crawled toward Ilyannha as though the light were their salvation.

"Back!" she whispered throatily, holding her bleeding hands to them in protest.

Seconds passed like hours. When her breathing steadied, she held the splinter of wood to the light. The splinter was less than a foot, but sharp as a dagger at the end.

She started to replace the splinter when the light revealed a signature of betrayal on the wood.

Her blood. *They will see the blood,* she thought.

Nearly giving in to panic, Ilyannha clenched her fists, allowing her mind to settle. Allowing her calm to return. A long moment passed, then she put the splinter to her mouth. Her mouth tasted of cotton, but she soon produced enough spittle to moisten the wood.

She gently rubbed the wood against her pants, using great care not to damage the fragile structure. Again she held the splinter to the light.

The blood was a smeared splotch.

She repeated the process. Ten minutes later, she had rubbed her blood from the wood.

Replacing the splinter, she returned to the group.

Sliding close, Brigitte asked, "Why are you so sure the commandos will come?"

Ilyannha took the blond Parisian's hands; the coolness of Brigitte's hands felt good against her own raw fingers. Then she told her young friend what she had known since being attacked by Kahlil.

"My government will never agree to their demands. The commandos will come. They must. Or we will all be killed."

Brigitte trembled. "What are we supposed to do when the commandos come to rescue us?"

Ilyannha squeezed Brigitte's hand. "We fight!"

40

BOULTON SACRETTE'S ATTENTION WAS GLUED TO the antiterrain radar scope on the *Seahawk*'s instrument panel. Occasionally he would pull back on the collective; or apply slight forward pressure, changing the altitude as necessary to stay beneath Libyan radar.

Skimming five feet above the desert, the Seahawk had left the sky above the sea six minutes before, turned to a one-ten heading, following a long natural depression carved into the earth by centuries of persistent wind.

Flanked by two hills stretching like long, sandy fingers, Sacrette kept the Seahawk in the slot, counting on the man sitting in the copilot seat as a backup against instrumentation error.

Through his night-vision mask Slattery saw nothing except an occasional bush jutting from the sand, or a rock formation standing in solitary prominence.

"There's the highway." Slattery's voice was calm, as though he were talking about something unimportant.

Running his finger along the red line on the map, he tapped the final destination lightly, then strained to see the natural outcropping rising above the desolate desert.

Seconds later, Sacrette heard the SEAL commander

betray his excitement with a loud shout. "Sabeh Tower!"

Slattery's arm was raised, pointing through the velvety blackness of the cockpit as though everyone else could see what only he could identify.

Sabeh-Tower—the Tower of Morning—was a promontory looming 300 feet; not significantly tall for a mountain, but where there was only desert, Sabeh Tower rose in singular grace.

"Hang on," Sacrette ordered over the interior commo system.

Easing the throttle back, Sacrette flared the helicopter at the base of the tower, holding the stick back until the skids made contact.

A swirl of dust rose like a windblown curtain, shrouding the helicopter in a cloud of swirling sand.

Cutting the power, Sacrette felt the helo settle into the sand. A sheen of perspiration covered his face, which was camouflaged in black.

"Let's move, " he ordered softly.

The Red Cell team moved in catlike silence, barely breaking the pristine silence of the desert night as they opened the door and slipped into the darkness.

A perimeter was established around the helo by Doc, Starlight, and Tico, while Sacrette, Deke, Gunny, and Phillips covered the *Seahawk* with camouflage netting.

Five minutes after landing, the team marched in single file, following Starlight, who was walking point.

Reaching the highway, the team lay in the darkness off the road.

"OK," Slattery whispered to Sacrette. "Let's try and get lucky." He scanned the east. There were no headlights moving on the highway. Turning to Tico, Deke ordered, "You know what to do. Get in position."

Tico slipped away from the group, threading his way

along the highway until his white-clad body was swallowed by the night.

"I hope this works," said Sacrette.

Slattery nodded. "It better. Otherwise, we're up shit creek in a chicken-wire boat."

Ten minutes passed. Fifteen. Nothing ventured along the highway toward Tobruk.

Trained in still positioning, the SEALs barely breathed; only Sacrette grew restless. His legs had begun to cramp and he was fighting the urge to move when he felt a nudge from Slattery, who was continuing his visual scan of the highway.

"Here comes the taxi service." Slattery spoke into a microphone connected to the assault harness under his Arab dress, "Get ready, Tico."

Snapping upright, Tico moved onto the highway, where he stretched out lengthways on his side. Beneath him, his hand gripped an automatic pistol equipped with a silencer.

From the east, two headlights pierced the night; the high pitch of the engine sounded like a sewing machine running out of control.

"Get ready," Slattery ordered the SEALs. Quietly, The Red Cell team spread along the highway.

The Red Cell team carried Uzis as well as automatic pistols, all equipped with sound-suppression silencers.

Deftly, they switched off the safety switches. Not a sound was heard as the filed safeties armed the deadly weapons for action.

The truck neared, its headlights proceeding in two narrow, white beams of light. As the vehicle passed the team's position, Sacrette breathed a sigh of relief.

It was a lorry. Large enough for the seven men.

Slattery took a deep breath, then waited; momentarily, he heard what he knew was the linchpin to their plan of getting into Tobruk.

The truck squealed to a halt.

Two men jumped from the truck, talking excitedly among themselves as they dashed to Tico, who lay motionless on the highway, his white-clad body illuminated in the light beaming from the headlights.

The Arabs appeared in the wash; one stooped, turning Tico's body over.

Sacrette saw the first man suddenly stiffen, then heard the muffled cough of the silencer.

The second man started to run. Another cough, this one from Sacrette's side.

Slattery sat framed between Sacrette and the field of light. In his hand, his pistol vented a telltale wisp of smoke that trailed from the muzzle into the night.

"Let's move." Sacrette heard no emotion in the deadly SEAL's voice.

Silent and fast, the bodies were quickly dragged off the road where they were unceremoniously covered with sand.

Sacrette took the wheel with Slattery sitting in the front; the rest of the Red Cell team piled into the back as the lorry sped off toward Tobruk.

Seconds later, the desert night covered the ground where the two dead Arabs lay buried.

To the west, the red taillights of the lorry burned brightly, then faded altogether.

Toward Tobruk!

41

0430.

CAPTAIN ELROD LORD SAT ERECT IN HIS CAPTAIN'S chair, his ears tuned to the MC-1 intercom. Beside him, Lt. j.g. Karl Jhabour was occupying his hands and mind with a Rubick's Cube.

Jhabour, of Lebanese descent, always carried the cube when summoned to the bridge by Captain Lord. It allowed him to while away the long, boring hours while listening to the radio, waiting to interpret for the battle group commander. He had been the interpreter when the *Valiant* cruised offshore from Beirut, during the Persian Gulf, and on several occasions near the Gulf of Sidra.

Interphased with the MC-1, satellite scan intercepted numerous frequencies used by the Libyan police and military installations near Tobruk, bringing the transmissions into the bridge.

"Anything?" Lord asked Jhabour.

Jhabour twisted the cube; the red squares fell into place on one side of the Rubick. Smiling, he replied, "Nothing. Except a fire call in the dhafeer district."

Lord massaged his face; the fatigue from the past four days had become acidic, wearing at his endurance and mental processes.

The physical deprivation he could handle; the mental drain was his concern. Had he made the right decision? Was the decision based on good military judgment; or had he placed seven good men and his military reputation in irreconcilable jeopardy?

He could handle the concerns of his career; it was the fate of the seven men that gnawed at his conscience.

He took a folder from his briefcase, opened the jacket, and stared at the face of a stranger.

The faxed record of Martin Thornson revealed much about the man before he moved to Libya: birth, childhood, military service. It was at that point that the record offered little about the man who could easily hold the fate of Lord, Sacrette, Red Cell Six, and twenty-four children in the palm of his hand.

Lord spoke to the face staring back at him from inside the jacket. "I wonder, Sergeant Thornson. On which side of the fence does your loyalty lie?"

Running his finger along Thornson's faxed DD-214, he noted that the airman had earned the Silver Star in Viet Nam, and the Purple Heart during the Tet Offensive.

"A brave man," Lord whispered. Then he thought of his men, and added, "I hope your love for your country runs as deep as your courage."

42

MARTIN THORNSON LAY ON HIS BACK, WATCHING HIS wife's still image reflect off the mirrored ceiling above his waterbed. When he felt her move, a wave rippled along his body, sending a bolt of excitement into his loins.

Turning over, he ran one of his large black fingers along her breasts, across her stomach, to the furry patch below her navel. Stroking her softly, he reflected on the pleasure and friendship she had provided him over the years. Not to mention five children.

Noting the familiar smile that moved her lips, he kissed her gently, then felt her arms close around him, drawing him into her waiting love.

They made love as the sun crawled through the window and onto the waterbed. Then he rose and walked to the bathroom. After showering, he made tea in the Arab tradition, pouring the hot brew from one glass to another, then repeating the process. Afterward, he stepped onto the veranda of his lavish home on the outskirts of Tobruk.

Sitting beside the swimming pool, as he did every morning, he watched the last traces of night begin to flee from the sun, which now rested at the top of a stone wall surrounding his backyard.

Following the fence, his eyes examined the courtyard, which was beautifully landscaped in Polynesian; palm trees stood sentinellike behind a rose garden. Hedges lined the south wall, giving the enclosed yard a sense of openness.

It was while he was draining the last of his tea that his eyes narrowed on the hedges; a slight movement between the foliage and the stone wall.

His fists tightened as he saw the hedges move.

"Who are you?" he asked in Arabic.

A tall man stepped forward; his reply was in English. "My name is Major Andrew Slattery. United States Marine Corps."

Thornson sat rock solid as Sacrette and the Red Cell team materialized from behind the American officer.

Raising his glass, Thornson toasted. "I believe the appropriate greeting is 'Semper Fi.'"

43

"YOU'VE GOT TO BE KIDDING!" THORNSON'S HUGE arms swept around the courtyard, then he aimed a spear-like finger at his house. "Do you think I would jeopardize all this . . . and my family? To help you!"

"Not us," Sacrette replied. "Twenty-four innocent children."

Thornson's lips curled down. "Twenty-four children. Twenty-four strangers." He jerked his head to the house. "I've got a wife and five babies. They're worth more than two hundred and twenty-four children."

"Your family won't be jeopardized, Sergeant Thornson." Slattery's voice carried a hard edge.

"Bullshit!" Thornson's fists balled into two tongs. He appeared ready to fight all seven armed men with his bare hands.

Gunny stepped forward. "Hey, brother. What's your fucking problem?"

Thornson pointed at the marine. "Don't brother me, man. You come in here like thieves out of the night wanting me to risk the lives of my family. You're crazy! Do you know what would happen to me if they found you here?"

"You'd be executed." Sacrette hit the nail on the head.

"Yeah." Thornson flew into a rage. "Along with my wife and children! You motherfuckers!"

"Don't motherfucker us, motherfucker." Gunny snapped his Uzi in Thornson's face. "We ain't got time to play games. We got business and you're our only hope, which don't look like much from where I stand."

"From where you stand? Shit. You don't know where you stand." Thornson looked at the Americans with contempt. "This is the dark side of the moon... that's where you're standing." He shook his head. "Man, I have a family in Qaddafi's government. Good family. You've put us all on the chopping block."

"Come on, Deke," Tico spoke, keeping his distance from the big expatriate. "Let's ice this mother and sky out of here. He's just a chickenshit turncoat who don't care about nothing but himself."

The Red Cell team took a provocative step forward, only to be stopped by the icy voice of their leader. "At ease, God dammit! We're not here to kill Americans."

It was Sacrette who spoke next, bringing a new clarity to the discussion. "Mr. Thornson, we understand your situation. We understand your concern for your security, and the security of your family. What you're failing to grasp is this simple fact: We're here. We have a job to do and we don't intend to leave because of your reluctance. We're going to find those children, with or without your help." His memory flashed the fax copy of Thornson's service record, and looking around at the opulence of his home, Sacrette put the situation into a perspective he hoped Thornson could understand.

"You're a retired member of the US military. You receive a sizable retirement check from our government, deposited monthly in the Bangue Nationale in Tobruk. A check that allows you to live like a king in splendid surroundings."

"What are you getting at, God damn you." His face revealed that he already knew Sacrette's meaning.

"Simple. You don't help . . . Uncle Sam jerks the check. You can try to live off what you make at the oil refinery, which, I daresay, isn't enough to maintain your current status."

Thornson shook his head. "You're bluffing."

Sacrette smiled slyly. "I don't bluff. You're retired military. Which means you can be recalled to active duty at any time by the President of the United States. Who, by the way, did so last night shortly before midnight. To put it in simple terms . . . you're back in the saddle again, Sergeant."

Slattery jumped on the lie, then added his own caveat. "Failure to comply with a presidential directive is a court-martial offense. You'll be stripped of your retirement, citizenship, and left to the gratitude of the Libyan government."

A wry smile filled Thornson's face. "They might be more grateful than you think. I'd say you boys are worth a pretty sizable piece of money."

Sacrette laughed. "You'd never live to spend the bounty. Much less prove your innocence to the government who, no doubt, will consider your family traitors."

Slattery stepped forward, telling Thornson, "Like the man says on television . . . 'Let's make a deal.'"

Thornson thought for a long moment. He sighed heavily, then asked, "What's the deal?"

Slattery motioned for Sacrette to close the bargaining. "You know your way around Tobruk. You've got contacts, people you can talk to without drawing attention. All we need is the location. Once you get us close to the location . . . you're out of the picture."

Thornson wasn't convinced that his end of the deal was that simple. Not to mention the fact that they had avoided one important possibility. "What if they find you here?"

"No way. We'll be with you."

"What if we're caught?"

Slattery responded with what the Red Cell team knew before the mission began. "You'll be on your own. As for us . . . they won't take us alive. You can tell the Libyans you were forced at gunpoint."

Thornson mulled over the offer. Another hitch presented itself. Pointing to Sacrette, Thornson asked, "What about him? You SEAL team boys might be willing to die with your guns smoking, but the jet jock here might bail out. If he's captured, he'll talk. You know they can make a man give up anything."

Slattery shook his head. "He won't be captured."

"How's that?" Thornson felt his stomach tighten.

"He'll be here . . . waiting for you to bring a message from me."

"What about my family?" Thornson didn't have to ask; somehow he already knew the answer.

Slattery's voice was colder than a blizzard. "Commander Sacrette will be responsible for your family."

44

"CAN WE TRUST THAT MAN, MAJOR?"

"It's not a question of trust. Besides . . . we don't have any choice," Slattery replied to Gunny, who was leaning forward from the rear of Thornson's van. Both men were watching Thornson say good-bye to his wife.

"How do you figure the man?" Gunny shook his head in true bewilderment. "How could an American live in this shithole of a country? After everything Qaddafi has done to America?"

Watching Thornson kiss his wife tenderly on the cheek, Slattery saw Gunny's question answered. "Some men don't need a country. They just need a place to live. It looks like she and his children are all the country he needs."

"Let's hope he keeps that thought close to his heart, Major. Otherwise, our butts are going to be hanging over a red-hot fire."

"It's not our butts I'm worried about, Gunny."

Thornson slid into the right-side driver seat. Without saying a word, he shoved the shift lever into reverse, backed out, and drove off, leaving a twisting funnel of loam-colored dust in the van's wake.

"Where do we start?" Slattery asked.

Thornson pointed to the city of Tobruk, which was visible against the blue horizon of the Mediterranean. "I know a man who keeps an ear close to the ground. If anyone knows, it'll be Karim Yamanni. He's a merchant in the bazaar."

"How much will it cost?" asked Slattery.

Thornson looked at Slattery with a contemptuous smile. "How much have you got?"

"That's not the question. How much will it cost?"

Thornson gave the question some momentary thought. "I figure about five thousand dollars. Did you boys bring your traveler's checks?"

Slattery jerked his head quickly. "We can handle that with no problem."

A deep-throated chuckle seeped from Thornson. "That's the least of your problems." He was pointing up the highway.

Slattery looked quickly, spotting the Libyan checkpoint, then turned to the rest of the team sitting in the rear of the van. "Keep your heads down. We're about to get up close and personal."

Slattery slipped into the back with the other SEALs, drawing a makeshift curtain hastily made to separate the front from the back. Their weapons were poised on the rear door.

From beneath his Arab garb, Gunny leveled his Uzi at Thornson's massive upper torso. "One slip, brother. One wrong move. And you're yesterday's news."

Thornson grunted as he downshifted the van.

As they approached the Libyan military checkpoint, Gunny noted two guards standing in front of a machine-gun position. Inside the sandbagged gun emplacement, two more soldiers lounged behind a Goryunov .51-caliber heavy machine gun.

"Let me do the talking," was all Thornson said.

"Since I don't speak Arabic, that might not be a bad idea," Gunny replied, his hand closed around the pistol grip of the Uzi hidden beneath his Arab dress.

"Good morning, Yassouf," Thornson greeted the first soldier familiarly. The tall, gangling black Libyan sergeant flashed Thornson a yellow-toothed smile.

"Good morning, my friend. Not working today?" Yassouf leaned against the door; his dark eyes were gazing past the expatriate to Gunny.

Thornson shook his head. "Taking the day off. My friend and I are going to the camel tournament in el-Karamha."

The soldier's nose pinched up. "Such a smelly place. And the noise is worse than the howl of the sirocco. I would prefer the women in the casbah. They don't smell much better . . . but they give a better ride."

Thornson laughed heartily. "I already have a good woman. What we want is to see a good camel fight."

Yassouf returned his gaze to Gunny. "Who is this one?"

"My wife's cousin," Thornson replied automatically.

Yassouf studied Gunny, who grinned at him. Momentarily, the guard stepped back, then waved his arm at Thornson. "Have a prosperous day."

"All days are prosperous, my friend." Thornson pressed the accelerator. The van sped off toward the city.

Gunny released a long sigh. "You handled that pretty good, brother."

Thornson drove without speaking. Fifteen minutes

later, the van threaded its way through the teeming traffic of downtown Tobruk. Exiting from Qaddafi Ring, the van was soon slowed by the ebb and flow of human traffic that began as they neared the bazaar.

"There's the bazaar." Thornson nodded to a broad street crowded with shops, pushcarts, fruit and vegetable stands, all of which appeared to swim within an undulation of humanity.

"God almighty," Gunny breathed nervously. "How are we going to get through that mess in this van?"

Thornson laughed. "With boldness...and panache!" He pressed the accelerator, sending the van toward the human sea.

Like the Red Sea before Moses, the crowd parted as the van approached. Within minutes the vehicle was swallowed up, its location in the crowded street marked by the bobbing of heads where the shoppers fled for their lives from the oncoming van.

Reaching the heart of the bazaar, Thornson pulled into an alley that was nothing more than a narrow cleft between two buildings.

"We're here." Thornson pointed at a side door of one of the buildings. "You sit tight. I'll see what I can find out." Thornson started to get out but was pulled back by Gunny's firm grip at his elbow.

"Not likely, brother. Where you go...I go," Gunny snapped.

Thornson's mouth twisted upward into a scowl. "Be cool, man. Remember...you're only 'passing.' And you're not a very convincing act. Besides, I got too much at stake."

"Major?" Gunny called through the curtain. "We got a situation."

Slattery stuck his head through the curtain. His face

was streaked with sweat from the heat in the stifling rear compartment.

"I heard." Slattery wiped at a rivulet of sweat running from his forehead. He looked hard at Thornson, then warned, "Let him go. If he goes dirty on us... we'll have hell to pay. But he's got more on the table than all of us."

Thornson opened the door, mumbling, "I heard that."

Gunny watched Thornson disappear through the adjacent side door. Ten minutes later, the retired American master sergeant returned.

"He wants six thousand dollars. Cash." Thornson was leaning through the window, speaking to Gunny.

"Six grand, Major," Gunny called through the curtain. The marine studied Thornson. "Can we trust him?"

Thornson shrugged. "What's to trust. I pay him for the information."

"Will he turn us over?"

Thornson shook his head slowly. "I told him I would kill him if he double-crossed me. He knows it's the truth. You can trust that."

Gunny turned to Slattery's hand, which was thrust through the curtain. The SEAL's fingers clutched a handkerchief tied in a knot.

Gunny took the handkerchief and handed it to Thornson, who immediately noticed the weight. Laying the handkerchief on the seat, Thornson untied the knot, spread the handkerchief open, then released a sharp gasp.

"Christ. You boys travel in style." He was staring incredulously at thirteen solid gold ingots.

"We each carry six ingots. Each ingot is an ounce. It's what you might call our method of avoiding argument on the international currency exchange."

Thornson retied the handkerchief, then returned to the merchant's shop.

Five minutes had passed when the burly Thornson walked hurriedly to the van, climbed in without speaking, then started the engine.

"Did you get the location?" Gunny asked.

Thornson said nothing. He drove off with a sudden tromp onto the accelerator.

"Hey, man," Gunny asked angrily. "I asked you a question. Did you get the location?"

Thornson reached inside his shirt. He took the handkerchief and laid it on Gunny's lap.

"Shit," Gunny cursed, feeling the weight of the ingots still captured within the tied handkerchief.

"It's a bust, Major," Gunny called through the curtain.

A disappointed grumble rolled from behind the curtain.

"Not entirely," Thornson said, jerking the van to avoid hitting an old man leading a burro along the narrow street.

Thornson took a piece of folded paper from inside his shirt pocket. Handing the paper to Gunny, Thornson nodded at the folded page. "The treacherous bastard . . . he tried to up the ante."

Gunny unfolded the page. Arabic words were scrawled hastily onto the paper. Gunny tried to read the name, but couldn't make out the writing.

The name of the location was obscured by the rich thickness of fresh blood.

"Shit. What happened?" Gunny handed the paper to Slattery.

"I caught the fucker on the telephone."

Slattery glanced quickly at Gunny. To Thornson,

he asked, "Did you see the name of the location?"

Thornson grinned through a sullen mask. "Yeah. I got the location."

Slattery released a long, grateful sigh. "Good. Where are they located?"

Thornson shook his head angrily. "Not so fast, Major. You don't get anything from me until I get something from you."

Gunny understood. He took the handkerchief and dropped the gold ingots into Thornson's lap. "You got it, brother."

Thornson's angry eyes flashed across the space separating the two black Americans. "Fuck that little bit of gold. I just killed a man. I was seen by some of his people. The police will be all over me in an hour. All because of you motherfuckers, and your goddamned patriotism!"

Gunny's Uzi lifted like a snake from beneath his Arab dress. "Alright, man. What do you want?"

Thornson's big fist slammed the dash. "I need out, man. Out. And you're my ticket. I know the location. That's what I'm dealing. You get me and my family out of this place, to wherever the hell you come from. Then I'll give you the location."

"Is that all?" Slattery asked in disbelief.

Thornson shook his head. "No way, man. I want more. I want it all. All or nothing. The way this has turned out . . . I got nothing to lose."

"How much?" Slattery motioned at Gunny to lower the weapon.

"Five hundred thousand dollars in a Swiss bank account. And seven fresh American passports for me and my family."

45

1015.

STANDING AT THE LARGE PLATE-GLASS WINDOW, SA-
crette looked through binoculars, maintaining constant
surveillance of the approach road leading to Thornson's
driveway.

Heat waves were already rising off the harsh terrain,
but the air-conditioning in Thornson's home made him
feel exceptionally comfortable. That was on the outside;
inside, he was a mass of twisted nervousness.

The nervousness had begun to heighten ten minutes
earlier as an armored tank column appeared on the highway leading east from Tobruk.

Eight Soviet-built TU-72 tanks were strung out in
a long clanking, rumbling formation, their antennae
whipping wildly as the column thundered along the highway.

"Damn," he cursed. The convoy was moving in the
same direction that they would have to travel to reach
the helo at Sabeh Tower.

Gradually, the convoy faded from sight, shifting Sacrette's concentration from the tanks to a fresh thought
materializing in his brain.

As he raised his binoculars to the north, the Mediterranean spread to the horizon in blue-green opales-

cence. However, for the first time in memory, the sea didn't appear beautiful. Rather, it stood as an awesome obstacle that kept stabbing him with the obvious question: How would they get back to the *Valiant*!

Before he could answer, the steady groan of an engine began to draw closer, and moments later Thornson's van appeared.

Thornson parked in the garage, lowered the heavy electric door, then slapped the side of the van with the flat of his hand.

The Red Cell team emerged, drenched in sweat, each man pulling at his Arab garb as they walked uninvited toward the pool.

They hit the water in six loud, voluminous explosions, sending water splashing over the edge where Thornson stood watching with obvious disdain.

"Perhaps I should bring you boys a cold beer," Thornson asked sarcastically.

Slattery pulled himself up to the edge of the pool, shading his eyes against the hot morning sun. "I suggest you get your family ready to travel, Mr. Thornson. No luggage. Not even a toothbrush. We'll be leaving in fifteen minutes."

Thornson smirked, then disappeared into the house.

Sacrette approached carrying his aviation map, asking, "Why is he getting his family ready to travel?"

Slattery explained the situation.

"Christ," Sacrette mumbled, looking off toward the highway. "This is turning into a clusterfuck."

Pulling himself out of the water, Slattery could see from Sacrette's face that there was a problem.

After hearing about the tank column, the wiry SEAL motioned the team out of the water. The SEALs stood around Slattery and Sacrette, who sat in lounge chairs.

Slattery peered at the Mediterranean. Finally, he released a despondent sigh. "That's a helluva long swim, Boulton."

Sacrette nodded in agreement. "It's too risky to go back for the helo. Security around that column will be tighter than a whale's ass underwater. There's no telling what we might run up against."

Slattery agreed, then asked, "Any suggestions?"

Sacrette nodded slowly; the muscles in his jaw worked tightly. "There's one way. It's risky, but at least it's a chance."

Slattery dabbed at his face with a towel. "Hell. We've been living on risk since we left the carrier. Tell me what you have in mind."

Sacrette explained his idea carefully. Slattery listened without comment. When Sacrette finished, the SEAL leader took the map from Sacrette.

Slattery studied the map for several seconds, then made a decision. "Bring Thornson."

Gunny hurried off toward the house.

Thornson joined the group wearing a suspicious expression. He repeated what they already knew. "My wife told me about the Libyan tanks."

"That changes the situation, Mr. Thornson." Sacrette held up the map; one finger pointed at a small village on the coast. "Can you get us to this village?"

Thornson looked at the name of the village. "Ramla. It's a fishing village."

Sacrette grinned. "Right. A fishing village. A fishing village filled with boats."

Thornson's eyes widened as the realization suddenly struck home. "You're crazy."

Sacrette grinned again. "That's why it'll work."

46

THORNSON'S VAN MAINTAINED A SAFE DISTANCE from the armored column, whose steady march east was clearly marked by a continuous cloud of billowing dust and smoke. South of Ramla, the van turned onto a dusty road that was little more than a trail; the deep ruts carved into the hard ground tested the strength of the tires while the suffocating heat tested the will of the travelers.

The Red Cell team sat in the rear with a child in each lap, except Slattery and Sacrette, who were crunched close together in the front.

Thornson drove mostly in silence, saying little, while making sullen gestures through the rearview mirror at the Americans who had turned his world upside down.

Reaching a rise, where the terrain emptied into a long incline leading to the village, Thornson stopped the van.

"Ramla," he said, pursing his lips toward the village.

"Christ," Slattery mumbled. "What a shithole."

Thornson laughed mechanically. "What did you expect? Carmel by the sea? With Clint Eastwood waiting to greet you with piña coladas?"

"I expected a fishing village with boats. Not a pisshole on the edge of hell," Slattery replied angrily.

"There're boats, Major. You'll see. There're boats. Not luxury liners, or aircraft carriers. Fishing boats. I'll give you the guided tour."

Ramla was a squalid, sun-backed wart, blemishing what would have been a majestic view of the Libyan coast. Mud houses stood in ragged disrepair; all signs of life were missing, except a cur dog scratching fleas near what Sacrette judged was the pier.

"I don't like it," warned Slattery. "Too damned quiet. It looks like an ambush."

Thornson broke in, pointing to the tallest building in the village. The white spire of a mosque jutted above the smaller structures. "It's noon. All the Moslems are at prayer."

"Thank God for Allah," chuckled Sacrette, who continued to scrutinize the village through binoculars.

There were only two signs of modernity: a fading Exxon sign hanging off kilter from a pole above the only wooden structure, a decaying shack Sacrette figured had once been a petrol station.

And a sleek, thirty-six-foot fishing boat rocking lazily offshore from a small, antiquated fleet of fishing dhows moored to the pier.

"There's the ticket home." Sacrette pointed at the fishing boat. The name *Khartoum* was painted across the transom.

"How do you want to make the play, Boulton?" Slattery asked.

"Arabs shy away from authority. If we act like we own the place, nothing will be said." Sacrette scanned the village, roaming the roofs of each structure. "I don't see any antennae. It's doubtful there's a radio transmitter in the entire village."

Slattery pointed at the *Khartoum*. "There's an antenna running up from the flying bridge."

Sacrette focused on the deck of the *Khartoum*. It was void of movement or activity. "Nothing on deck," he said, then stopped abruptly as something slid into view from the windward side of the boat. "Hold everything."

A small johnboat was tied to the stern.

"Let's go to the pier, Mr. Thornson," Sacrette ordered.

The van lumbered down the hill to the village, where the pungent odor of fish drying from a shed was strong enough to peel paint. At the pier, which was nothing but a rickety platform made of decaying boards, the van eased to a halt.

Sacrette motioned toward the *Khartoum*, telling Slattery, "You and Tico swim underwater to the windward side of the boat. Have Tico bring back the johnboat for the children. You secure the interior of the boat. I don't have to tell you we can't let anyone get to that radio."

Slattery understood and motioned for Tico to follow. Slattery and the stout Mexican climbed out of the van, stripped off their clothing, then slid into the water.

"Let's hope these Arabs enjoy praying for long periods of time, Mr. Thornson."

Thornson looked around distastefully. "It don't look like there's anything else for entertainment. They won't come up for air for another hour."

Three minutes later Tico had secured the johnboat and was paddling toward the pier. Slattery, who had disappeared inside the hull, came back on deck.

"She's clear," said Sacrette, watching the SEAL leader pat the top of his head.

Moving fast, the SEALs loaded their rucksacks and

weapons into the johnboat. After the children and Thornson's wife were loaded, the SEALs swam to the *Khartoum* while Thornson paddled the johnboat.

"Can you start this lady?" Sacrette asked Slattery.

"Piece of cake," he replied.

"Good. Let's get under way."

The noise of the engines starting ripped the tranquility of the tiny harbor with a gigantic gurgle that bled into a steady drone as Slattery eased the throttles forward.

It was then, when the SEAL leader was about to engage the transmission to forward, that a loud shout pierced the steady drone.

"*Alto!*" the voice commanded in Italian.

Sacrette looked over his shoulder. A lone figure wearing a scuba cylinder and shorty wetsuit was standing on the stern ladder. One hand gripped the edge of the ladder; the other gripped a pneumatic speargun.

Carefully, the diver climbed into the boat. The deadly barb of the spear shaft was aimed at Boulton Sacrette.

Sacrette didn't hesitate. Instinctively, he threw out his left foot, striking the figure in the stomach. The weapon fired, sending the deadly bolt toward Slattery, who miraculously ducked as the barb splintered the wood above the wheel.

Shoving the throttles forward, Slattery yelled to Phillips. "Take him down."

The *Khartoum* lurched forward, throwing the man momentarily off balance.

In the split second that followed, Phillips drew his Sykes-Fairburn knife and extended his arm in a single sweeping move. The deadly dagger found its mark in the diver's larynx.

The man's facemask filled with his protruding eyes;

blood spewed as his hands pulled the knife from his throat.

Dropping to his knees, the diver pitched forward, twisted on the deck, then fell still.

"Nice move." Slattery winked at Phillips.

The tall SEAL said nothing; he cleaned the blood from the blade with a quick wipe against the dead man's wetsuit.

Slattery looked at the instrument panel, then caught Sacrette's attention.

"Our fuel tanks are drier than Kelsey's nuts."

Sacrette judged they had about thirty minutes of running fuel. "Hell of an irony, Deke. Here we are in one of the biggest oil-producing countries in the world, and we're flat-assed out of gas."

Slattery shrugged. "Do we risk giving up our location?"

Sacrette took the microphone, then tuned in a radio frequency on the transmitter. "We don't have any choice." He took a deep breath, then keyed the mike. "Home Plate . . . this is Thunderbolt. Transmitting in the clear on one-twenty-one-five."

The sound of Boulton Sacrette's familiar voice brought the *Valiant*'s communications officer to his feet with resounding speed.

"Roger, Thunderbolt. Home Plate copies on one-twenty-one-five. Read you five-by-five. Report position."

There was a strained pause, followed by Sacrette's sarcastic reply. "Hell, son, if I knew my position I wouldn't be bothering you. Get a fix on my signal and send some help. Tell the Umpire we're bringing back the Holy Grail."

The commo officer glanced to a young radar specialist sitting nearby. He turned a thumbs-up to the officer.

"Roger, Thunderbolt. Have fixed your position. Suggest you do not transmit unless essential. You are transmitting from inside Libyan territorial waters."

"No shit, Dick Tracy!" came Thunderbolt Sacrette's response.

47

THE SMILING FACES OF BOULTON SACRETTE, DEKE Slattery, and the rest of the Red Cell team nearly brought tears to the eyes of Captain Lord.

The *Khartoum* had been spotted by Sea Rescue within thirty minutes of the transmission. The boat was scuttled by Slattery, who dropped a hand grenade into the flying bridge while leaning from the rescue helo.

What brought the grimness to his momentary joy were the demands placed on the occasion by Martin Thornson.

Captain Lord disapproved of blackmail; however, the exigence of the situation allowed Thornson to dictate his terms with considerable leverage.

Thornson remained aboard the *Valiant*, where he awaited a telephone call from his wife signaling that she and the children had arrived safely at the American air base in Heraklion, Crete.

"Here's your thirty talons of silver, Mr. Thornson." Captain Elrod Lord approached Thornson in the ready room, where the expatriate had been sequestered since arriving aboard the carrier. Handing Thornson a computer printout, the captain watched the retired serviceman with a steady, contemptuous gaze. "We've kept our word. It's time for you to keep yours."

Thornson ignored the gaze, and its meaning. Taking the paper excitedly, he read the communiqué from Jules Barclay, the manager of Suisse Credit bank, Zurich, Switzerland:

Deposited under the name of Martin Thornson, the sum of five hundred thousand United States dollars.

Thornson released a long, slow whistle. "Yeah, baby. Five hundred yards. I can buy a lot of distance between me and the Libyans with this, Captain Lord."

Folding the confirmation, he shoved the receipt into the right pocket of the navy dungaree shirt he was wearing. From the left pocket, he took the page stained with Yamanni's blood.

Lord motioned Thornson to the front of the ready room. "If you'll please accompany the ensign."

Thornson followed the communication officer to the bank of television sets depicting a variety of topographical photographs transmitting from the *LaCrosse* satellite.

In the first set, the copper-white buildings of Tobruk shined along the northern Libyan coast. Another television screen portrayed a broader photograph of the East Libyan topography.

Pointing to the second set, Thornson said, "They've been taken out of Tobruk. They're east of the city, on the coast near the Egyptian border."

"Specificity, Mr. Thornson. Do you have the name of the village?"

Thornson shook his head. "They're not in a village. They're in a villa built during the Italian occupation. Villa de Valentino. The Libyans use it for entertaining high-ranking officers, and out-of-country guests. If you get my drift."

Lord recognized the name from previous intelligence reports; the villa had been cited as a potential target in 1985 when the United States launched a retaliatory bombing raid against Qaddafi for assisting terrorists in killing American servicemen in Berlin.

Lord opened his briefcase, thumbed through a thick stack of papers, then pulled out a single sheet. He handed the sheet to the ensign sitting at the computer console.

"Punch in these coordinates, then zoom *LaCrosse* to maximum amplification."

The ensign punched the coordinates into the computer, pressed ENTER, then sat back. Moments later the screen blurred; another few seconds passed.

The color screen turned beige.

The ensign nodded at the screen. He was grinning as he said, "*LaCrosse* is photographing the ground around an area measuring approximately one square yard."

"Back the amplification off to five thousand feet," Lord ordered.

The ensign pressed more buttons. The screen seemed to move as the satellite hovering eighty miles above the Libyan coast decreased photographic amplification.

On the screen, a white blur now sat within the beige field; the top of the beige field was bordered with a fringe of blue.

"Five thousand feet," the ensign reported.

Lord leaned to the screen, "Clarify."

The ensign pushed more buttons linking the console to the satellite's photographic equipment.

Gradually, the white clarified, revealing to Lord what he recognized unmistakably as the Villa de Valentino.

"The villa is surrounded by desert on the east, west, and south," he said calmly, running his finger over the beige area. Touching the blue fringe at the top of the screen, he added, "This is the Mediterranean."

From the air, the villa was a quadrangle in outline; what appeared to be an open courtyard lay at its center. Parked in the center of the courtyard was the clear image of a helicopter. Nothing unusual.

What made Lord curious was the sprinkling of rectangular objects spread around the outer perimeter of the villa.

Touching one of the rectangles, Lord ordered, "Take *LaCrosse* in tighter. I'm particularly interested in these rectangularly shaped objects. Bring one up to full clarity."

The ensign pressed more buttons. The terrain seemed to race toward Lord, who watched one of the rectangular objects grow until its detail erased all doubt about its identity.

"Damn," Lord cursed softly.

Thornson grumped unenthusiastically, "In case you're wondering, Captain Lord, I saw that big mother lumbering past my house this morning. That's a TU-72."

Lord recognized the design of the TU-72 Soviet built tank. "So that's where they were going," he said while reaching for the telephone. To the executive officer on the flag bridge, Lord barked, "Wake up Commander Sacrette and Major Slattery. I need to see them ASAP in the ready room."

"What's your next move, Captain?" Thornson asked. He was swelled up like a croaking frog.

Lord left the room for a moment. When he returned,

four large Marine SPs followed carrying automatic weapons.

"Secure this man," Lord ordered smuggly.

Thornson's eyes bulged as the SPs gripped his arms.

"I may have to assist you in extortion for the children's welfare," Lord began calmly. "I may have to assist you with resettlement. But, by God, I'll not have you strutting around my ship until you can be properly transported to Crete."

"What the hell!" Thornson tried to twist away from the SPs, but they were too overpowering.

"Put him in the brig!" Lord commanded.

A smile crawled across Lord's mouth for a split second, then the worry returned as he looked back at the Soviet tank.

48

FIFTEEN MINUTES LATER, SACRETTE WAS STANDING in front of the television screen beaming the image of a single TU-72 armored tank. Slattery stood looking over his shoulder; both men were dressed in fatigue shorts and tank-top T-shirts.

Neither man appeared especially disturbed by the Russian tank.

"Laser-guided SMART bombs," Sacrette said emphatically. "We'll surgically excise the tanks on a 'mud run.' They'll be out of the picture before the popcorn starts to pop."

Slattery nodded appreciatively. "I sure hope so. We're not going to have time to socialize with tanks."

Lord appeared pleased. "Excellent. My thoughts exactly." He turned to the ensign, ordering, "Let's have a side-looking scan of the villa."

Seconds later, *LaCrosse* was projecting a side view of the villa, giving the men their first view of where the children were being held hostage.

"The layout's simple enough," Slattery commented. "The quad shape gives them four points of primary defense."

At each corner, a redoubt protruded from the structure. Slattery pointed at one of the redoubts forming the junctures of the villa. "Let's take a closer look at the redoubts."

The ensign zoomed onto one of the redoubts over-looking the Mediterranean.

A single figure could be seen standing at an opened window facing out from the redoubt. The camera revealed a layer of sandbags rising above the base of the window frame. Sitting on top of the sandbags, the long, twin outlines of a deadly defender caught Slattery's attention. On closer examination, he spoke to the screen. "They've got the seaside covered with Ultimax 100s. State-of-the-art light machine guns, sports fans."

Lord said nothing; nor did Sacrette. Both naval aviators observed that Slattery was being drawn into that special mental state of study a tactician must reach to acquire the "feel" of his objective.

The SEAL ran his finger along the redoubt facing into the Mediterranean. Giving the figure standing behind the sandbags a light tap, he said to the ensign, "Let's have a side view of the south wall."

The south wall filled the screen. A smooth wall twenty feet high joined the two redoubts. Four windows could be seen, each framed by heavy metal bars.

Slattery pointed to one of the windows. "Zoom in on this window. The third window from the east."

LaCrosse gave a detailed view of the window.

Looking at Sacrette, Slattery asked, "Do you see anything distinctive about this particular window?"

Sacrette examined the window, then commented on the obvious distinction. "The window is boarded over."

"Yes," Slattery agreed.

Sacrette looked at Slattery. His eyes reflected the

meaning of the distinction. "That's where they're keep-ing the hostages?"

"Affirmative."

"How are you going to get to them?" Captain Lord asked cautiously.

Slattery didn't answer; instead, he snapped an order to the ensign. "Give me a full view of the east wall."

The wall came into full view. Slattery studied the screen intently. Finally, his eyes narrowed on a particular feature. Looking at Lord, he said flatly, "I'll need some information from your people in meteorology."

Lord picked up the telephone, dialed a number, and waited for a reply. "What information do you need, Major?"

Slattery stepped back from the screen. "The precise hour and minute when the moon will reach a twenty-degree angle on the villa's western horizon."

Drawn by his own curiosity, Sacrette stepped beside Slattery. He studied the east wall for several minutes while Lord passed the request on to the meteorologist at the opposite end of the telephone line.

Suddenly a grin spread across Sacrette's face. Turn-ing to Slattery, he spoke in a low voice, "You sly son-of-a-gun."

Before Slattery could reply, Captain Lord's voice offered the information the SEAL commander re-quested.

"Our meteorologist predicts the moon should reach that angle at precisely oh-three-twelve."

Slattery glanced at his watch, then to the two naval officers. "Coordinate your air strike to begin at oh-three-thirty. That's when the Red Cell team will take the villa."

"How do you plan to insert?" asked Lord.

"We'll take the helo to a point five miles offshore. Using scuba, we can make an underwater insertion onto the beach," Slattery replied.

"That's a long swim, Major Slattery." Lord knew the SEALs were in superb condition; however, five miles was a long swim, especially if combat was waiting.

Slattery had the answer. "No problem. We'll use Casper and the Friendly Ghosts. We can move fast, and avoid detection with their cover."

Sacrette and Lord both laughed.

"Where are they?" Sacrette knew the special unit known as Casper and the Friendly Ghosts were based at Coronado, California, headquarters for the Navy's SEAL training center.

"We had them flown to Rota as a contingency. They can be here in a few hours."

Pulling himself from deep thought, Lord spoke confidently. "Gentlemen, we'd better alert essential personnel. We have a lot to do if we're going to make this work." He picked up the telephone and dialed the number connecting him to the MC-1 internal intercom.

"Attention on the carrier. This is the captain. We are now at condition Zulu. Repeat. We are now at Zulu. All commanders and execs report to the main ready room for briefing."

Throughout the carrier, Captain Lord's voice had sent over 6000 men in motion with his alert order.

Sacrette felt the adrenaline surge; clapping his hands together loudly, he walked quickly from the ready room.

Five minutes later he found Farnsworth reading a *Playboy* magazine in the tool crib of the F-18 maintenance area.

"Get the birds ready, Chief," Sacrette ordered.

"What mode? Strike. Or fighter?"

"I want seven aircraft in the strike mode for bombing. Seven in fighter mode to provide CAP cover against Libyan fighters. I suspect once the balloon goes up, the Libs will get into the play."

Noting that there was still one aircraft without mode orders, Farnsworth asked the CAG, "What about your aircraft?"

Sacrette's eyes were shining as he replied, "Strike/Fighter!"

DAY FIVE

49

STANDING ON THE FLIGHT DECK OF THE USS *Valiant*, Major Deke Slattery wasn't staring toward the south, where the Villa de Valentino lay eighty miles away on the Libyan coast. His concentration was on the northwest, where the dull pulsation of rotor blades announced the gradual approach of a helicopter.

Walking toward Slattery, Sacrette could barely make out the outline of the Red Cell team. They stood beside Slattery, all dressed in black wetsuits, seeming to melt into the blackness of the early morning.

"Good morning," said Sacrette, who appeared fresh despite having had little sleep the past four days.

"Semper Fi," Slattery replied. The other SEALs merely acknowledged Sacrette with a casual glance while watching the helicopter approach.

A few seconds passed, then the landing lights of an H-53 Sea Stallion swept the flight deck. Standing in the wash of brilliant light, the SEALs appeared to shine as they marched briskly toward the helo while the heavy Sea Stallion settled onto the deck like a giant dragonfly.

The whirring of the rear ramp as it opened filled Sacrette with an overwhelming sense of exhilaration.

Sacrette had only heard of Casper and the Friendly

Ghosts. Now he would see the special warfare assist unit in the flesh.

Or in the fish—which seemed more appropriate.

Gunny hoisted a heavy rucksack on to his shoulder, then pointed to the helo with a sweep of his Uzi. "Let's saddle up."

The others followed. Sacrette walked with Slattery.

Stepping into the interior, Slattery saw three canvas vats lined up side by side. The sound of air exhausting from the vats beat a steady rhythym. Suddenly a flash of gray from the center vat sent water spilling over the side.

Gunny leaned over the vat, then stroked the creature lying submerged. "Casper is getting a hard on."

Another snort burst from one of the vats. Phillips stroked the gray body as though he were petting a favorite hunting dog.

"So this is Casper?" Sacrette knelt in front of the center vat. Reaching down, he ran his hand along the dorsal fin of the most beautiful porpoise he'd ever seen.

Doc touched the porpoise lying in the starboard side vat. "Hello, Saturn."

"What's this apparatus?" Sacrette asked, pointing to a strange pod mounted on Casper's head.

"Command and steerage pod. We call it the 'tickler.'" Slattery then explained the tickler. "A small receiver is implanted into Casper's brain. A signal is transmitted by satellite to a point along the course he's to follow. The receiver picks up the signal. Casper homes for the signal, the Friendly Ghosts follow."

"Like leading a goat with a carrot dangling from a stick?" asked Sacrette.

"Precisely. The signal will be directed by a commo officer in the CIC. Once we get to where we're going the signal will hold until the porpoise intercepts. Then he can be held on that point, or rerouted to another location."

"Interesting."

Slattery grinned. "That's not all. If the porpoises are picked up by enemy sonar, they'll mask our presence. We'll look like a school of porpoises."

"Beats the hell out of a long underwater swim," Gunny added.

"How do you hold on?" asked Sacrette, who was genuinely enthralled by the porpoise concept.

Slattery held a harness for Sacrette's perusal. Two hand grips were joined to the harness. "We slip this harness onto their bodies, then hold on to the hand grips."

Sacrette shook his head in amazement. "I'm impressed."

"You should be. The project didn't come cheap. These gentlemen are worth their weight in gold. Literally," Slattery added.

Sacrette checked his watch. He could see it was getting close to the SEALs' departure time. "Deke." He stuck out his hand. "I'll see you on the beach."

Slattery took his hand. He winked. "Don't be late, Thunderbolt."

Sacrette squeezed his hand reassuringly. "We'll be there. You know what to do once you've taken the villa."

Slattery nodded. "Hold until the marines arrive."

"Affirmative. They'll be heloed to assist in evacuation once you report the villa has been secured." He looked at Doc. "Doc, the medical team will be standing by on the *Valiant* to receive casualties. Don't leave anybody behind."

"What if we lose some people?" Doc asked flatly.

"Bring them out, Doc. Everybody goes home. Dead

or alive." With that final order Sacrette walked off the Stallion.

Two minutes later the black helo thundered from the deck of the *Valiant*.

Toward Libya!

50

THE VILLA DE VALENTINO STOOD IN MOON-WASHED splendor against the Arab night, as though it were carved from chalk. Protected by the sea on the north, and Libyan tanks on the remaining three sides, Abu Mohammad Jemal walked with an air of arrogance across the courtyard.

He paused beside the helicopter, a JetRanger, checked the doors to be sure they were unlocked, then climbed the stone steps quickly, heading straight for the redoubt on the northeast corner.

He found Awad leaning against the sandbags piled on the floor; a twin-barreled Ultimax machine gun rested in a gunport built into the protective barrier.

Glancing in, Jemal said nothing. He merely grunted approvingly at finding the Ashbal awake at his guardpost.

Continuing along the terrace overlooking the courtyard, he found Layla standing in front of the room housing the hostages.

She leaned against the door, listening. "They are quiet," she said.

"They are sheep," he replied. "Sheep are always quiet before the slaughter."

"Will they be slaughtered?"

He glanced at his watch. "The foolish Israelis are running out of time."

"Perhaps they are not taking us seriously."

An evil grin cut across his face. "They will take us seriously by the time you say your noon prayers."

She looked puzzled. "What are you planning?"

He spoke without emotion. "We will kill three hostages."

Layla looked pleased. "The Israelis?"

He shook his head. "No. I have other plans for them. The Israelis and the others will become useful in the future. Very useful."

From inside the room, Ilyannha Lavi listened quietly, her ear pressed hard against the door. Hearing Jemal, she felt a cold chill twist down her spine. She trembled slightly, then clutched her fists tightly, fighting back the fear.

"They will come. I know they won't leave us here to die," she whispered softly as she turned back to the room.

The children sat in three groups; each group was led by one of the Israeli children.

Except for the thin shaft of light seeping through the cracked board at the window, they had become accustomed to living in total blackness.

The day and night had not been spent idly; they had begun to prepare themselves for the chance of rescue. Exercise had made their muscles stronger; planning had given them mental encouragement.

Raanan, a junior black belt in karate, had taught the children how to use their fingers to strike at the eyes and throat. In small groups, they practiced with each other until the children could strike at a target by the feel of its presence.

Ilyannha sat on the floor, then softly called the group around her. She could feel an excitement from them; a sense of confidence.

"The terrorists' weapons are the Kalashnikov AK-47 assault rifles." She began describing the dreaded automatic weapon. "There are thirty bullets in the magazine."

"What is a magazine?" asked Brigitte.

"The magazine is the small box in front of the trigger. Next to the trigger, on the right side, is a safety switch. You must push the switch up in order to fire the weapon."

Raanan spoke up, telling them, "Close your eyes. Picture the weapon in your hands."

Each child closed their eyes and saw the weapon materialize.

Raanan continued, "It is very heavy, but you can hold it easier with the butt under your armpit. Do it."

The children slipped the butt of the imaginary weapon under their armpit.

"Hold the weapon by the pistol grip. With your left hand hold the wooden piece beneath the barrel. Use your right index finger to push the switch up until you feel it click twice."

The children raised their imaginary weapons, switched the safety to full automatic.

"Pull the trigger," Raanan ordered.

The darkness was too deep for anyone to see the broad grins stretching across the children's faces as they pulled the triggers, sending thirty deadly projectiles into their captors.

"This is fun," said a voice.

"I wish it were for real," said another.

Ilyannha's soft but firm voice followed, "It will be. Very soon."

"What if they don't come to rescue us?" asked a voice with a German accent.

Ilyannha looked to the split in the board where the needlelike splinter remained in place.

"We will have to rescue ourselves."

"When?" asked Brigitte.

Recalling the judgment of Jemal, she replied softly to the children who did not know that three were destined to die before noon. "When they bring our breakfast."

51

0200.

GUNNY LEANED OUT OF THE REAR RAMP OF THE SI-korsky H-53 Sea Stallion. The black helo hovered five feet off the prop-swathed water of the Mediterranean. The propwash felt cool against his face, which was streaked with sweat from the wetsuit covering his body.

"Prepare to insert Casper and the Friendly Ghosts!" Slattery shouted from behind.

Gunny turned to the interior of the Stallion. Sitting in webbed seats, the Red Cell team lined the two walls. Their weapons were strapped to their legs in waterproof gurneys. Fragmentation and stun grenades hung from harnesses beneath their diving backpacks.

Each man wore an SCRB-1, a prototype self-contained rebreathing unit; double hose regulators ran from the first stage that fed air from twin scuba tanks concealed within the hardshell plastic fairings on their backs.

The RB did what conventional scuba equipment was not designed to do: the unused air was recycled through a chemical CO_2 "scrubber" that allowed for maximum use of compressed air in the tanks. This allowed for greater bottom time while eliminating the telltale trail of bubbles left after exhalation from a conventional unit.

With the RB they could stay down longer and, more importantly, go undetected beneath the noses of the enemy.

Slattery took the mike and spoke to the pilot. "Give me fifteen degrees increase in the angle of attack."

As the nose came up, the helo's rear ramp sat only inches off the water.

"Helmets on," Slattery ordered, slipping a Superlite diving helmet over his head. The Superlite integrated the mask, regulator, and communications systems into one unit, giving the men the look of astronauts.

Gunny leaned to the front of Casper's tub. He gripped a zipper handle sealing the front of the tub.

From behind, Doc picked up the rear of the tub. "Ready on you," he called to Slattery.

"Insert Casper!" Slattery shouted.

Gunny pulled the zipper handle; the front of the tub opened. Simultaneously, Doc lifted the rear of the tub to his waist.

On a cushion of gorging water, Casper slid gracefully into the sea.

Free of the tub, Casper executed a front flip, then dashed around the helo, waiting for the Friendly Ghosts.

Jake and Saturn were next, followed by Slattery and the Red Cell team.

As the helo banked sharply, the roar of the engines filled the air for several seconds, then faded as the Stallion flew north, skimming five feet above the surface.

"Hook up!" Slattery ordered. To prevent loss of a man should his hand slip from the hand grips, each of them wore a five-foot static line extending from his harness. The connector links were attached to the collars worn by the porpoises.

Two men were assigned to each porpoise, and when

hooked up, the porpoises glided like gray ghosts beneath the surface, turning a long slow circle, Jake and Saturn following in a trail on the outside of Casper.

"Red Cell one to Red Cell team. Commo check." Slattery's voice crackled over the Superlite U/W commo system. The closed circuit commo system had a range of 400 meters; the frequency was known only to the team.

"Red Cell two. Go," said Gunny, who was hanging beneath Saturn.

"Red Cell three. Go," Doc replied from his position next to Gunny.

"Red Cell four. Go," hooked up to Jake, Tico spoke calmly to Slattery.

"Red Cell five. Go," next to Tico, Phillips piped in.

"Red Cell six. Go." Starlight, hanging from Casper, glanced at Slattery, who was connected to the opposite side of the porpoise.

Deke took a black transmitter from one of the pouches on his harness. He pressed a red switch, and a signal was intercepted by *LaCrosse*, then transmitted to the CRT aboard the carrier.

From the *Valiant*'s CIC, the technician manning the CRT noted a red blip as it appeared on the screen, depicting the precise position of the pod mounted on Casper's head.

"OK, big fellow," the technician whispered softly. "Let's go get the bad guys." He punched in the coordinates, then hit the transmit key. Instantly, the satellite transmitted a laser signal to a point approximately ten feet in front of Casper.

Inside the pod a receiver picked up the signal, sending a "tickling" sensation into the porpoise's brain.

Casper was now electronically "in tow," and could be guided in any direction desired by the technician.

Turning automatically to port, Casper began to glide smoothly through the water. Jake and Saturn wheeled on the lead porpoise's flanks.

Trailing beneath the surface, the SEALs used their hands as elevators, allowing themselves to glide like airplanes. This was necessary to conceal their presence when the porpoises periodically surfaced for air.

"Red Cell team . . . maintain radio silence," Slattery ordered.

Seconds later, the nine mammals moved like dark apparitions toward the beach beneath the Villa de Valentino.

52

ZENA NESHER SAT UP IN BED AS SACRETTE CAME toward her wearing a broad grin. It was the first time she had seen him since falling from the helo. She was glad Doc Holweigner had insisted on keeping her in traction rather than risk further injury that could occur during a seaborne medevac. It gave her the chance to see Sacrette one more time before returning to Israel.

Hurriedly, she tried to fix her hair but knew that was fruitless. Three days in a hospital bed could cause more disrepair to a woman's appearance than three months in the desert.

"Good morning. You look beautiful," Sacrette said. He leaned over and kissed her forehead.

"You're a wonderful liar," she replied.

He was dressed in his flight suit and speed jeans, and she immediately sensed that something was up. Was it the lateness of the hour? The way he was dressed? Or that characteristic swagger of the fighter pilot about to launch into action?

"Are you going . . . or returning?" she asked.

"Getting ready to go. I wanted to see you before I left. To let you know what's going on."

"What is going on?"

"The rescue mission has already begun. The SEALs are en route. We're scheduled for launch in thirty minutes."

"What are the chances of success?"

Sacrette shrugged. "Any rescue operation encounters a margin of risk. We anticipate twenty percent casualties."

She looked hard at Sacrette. "That's very high."

"Yes. The governments involved have considered the situation in the alternative and agree the terrorists must be stopped before we lose the initiative."

She understood. "Beirut?"

"Yes. If they don't kill the children, they'll probably be forced to move them to Beirut. In which case they'll be lost forever."

"What is the Israeli government doing about the demands?"

"They've offered to release all the political prisoners inside Israeli jails in exchange for the children. The terrorists have rejected the offer outright."

The reality of the situation swept over Zena like a wave. "They knew the price was too high from the beginning. Which means they never intended to exchange the hostages."

Sacrette shook his head. "Apparently not. They're going to use the children the way Hazbollah uses American hostages in Beirut. We expect they'll execute one or more to make their point, and while the world is in an uproar, they'll make a run for Beirut."

"Similar to the *Achilles Loro* hijacking."

Sacrette recalled the incident in which the Palestinian terrorists had hijacked a luxury liner, killing one hostage before getting safe passage in exchange for the hostages. Safe passage that was guaranteed by the Egyptians, but rescinded by the Americans after the murder of the hostage. "There's a difference. This time we won't be able to force the aircraft to land. They'll use the hostages as a shield."

Zena fell into deep thought. Finally, she spoke from her heart. "We seem destined to travel this road of continual destruction until there is nothing left. Israel was such a beautiful dream. Now, it's become a nightmare."

"A Viet Nam that never ends."

"Viet Nam? You could withdraw from Viet Nam. What are we to do?"

"I don't know the answer. If there is an answer."

"There is an answer. The question is whether we have the courage required to resolve the problem."

Sacrette thought he knew what she was saying. "Give the Palestinians autonomy? A political state?"

"Either that . . . or give them an equal share in the responsibility. The civil rights of all Palestinians have been suspended. Their land is being confiscated. How can we expect them to accept what we Israelis were not willing to accept from Hitler? In many ways we've become another apartheid state, similar to South Africa. We have more than ten thousand new immigrants a year. Mostly elderly Jews who want to live out their final years in the Holy Land. But we are losing nearly fifteen thousand a year due to emigration. Not the old, but the young. Our youth is leaving rather than stay and fight an endless war. One day we may become nothing but a nation of old people. Then, the Arabs will have us by the throat. It will have all been for nothing."

"I understand your feelings. At the same time, I understand their commitment to fight. If I was forced to live in Mexico as a refugee, or live in some occupied part of my country, I would fight with all my strength. It's the method they're using that's unconscionable. The means of terrorism does not justify the end. Not when it's directed at the innocent."

Zena sighed heavily. "One man's evil is another man's good. One man's terrorist is another man's patriot."

Sacrette stared at her for a long moment. "What about Zena Nesher? Where does she stand in the overall picture? Will she take her daughter and leave the kibbutz for the safety of another country?"

A proud smile filled her face. "Zena Nesher is Sabra. She has no other country. Nor does her daughter. We will stay. We will continue to fight if necessary. You see, we have as much to lose . . . as the Palestinians have to gain."

Sacrette took her hand. Changing the subject, he touched on what they both knew would happen next. "I understand you're to be medevaced to Tel Aviv."

"Yes. In a few hours."

He checked his watch. "I don't suppose I'll see you again."

She reached and took his face in her hands. "You'll see me . . . if that's what you want."

Sacrette kissed the palms of her hands. "I'd like that very much."

Their lips touched lightly. His arms came around her gently. They kissed for a long, warm moment. Finally, he pulled himself from her arms, and standing quickly, he started away.

"Shalom, Boulton Sacrette. May God go with you," she called softly.

"Shalom," he replied over his shoulder.

Then he was gone.

53

0315.

THE MOON HUNG TO THE WEST OF THE VILLA DE Valentino, paling the east wall where the shadows stretched in a long black swath toward a rocky cove.

The tide surge was heavy, pounding the beach with a constant assault of waves; it rolled in with the drama of an armored column charging across an open plain.

Twenty meters offshore, the SEALs approached in silence; clinging to the bottom, they allowed the current to push them forward until the water was shallow enough for them to see the outline of the moon beaming through from the surface.

Ditching their RBs, they floated to the surface, dragging their heavy equipment bags in tow.

Phillips was the first to come ashore. He slipped through the dark outcroppings of rock splitting sea from beach and set up in a craggy overhang. Sitting behind a SAW machine gun, he scanned the wall of rock leading to the villa, then looked back to the water where another black-clad figure emerged.

Moving in a low crouch, Slattery raced to Phillips, who silently disappeared, leaving Slattery to cover the remaining SEALs as they came ashore.

Phillips moved through the rocks like a mountain

goat until he reached the base of the villa in the shadows on the east wall. Raising a starlight scope to his eyes, he scanned the wall carefully, beginning at the corner as instructed by Slattery.

Almost immediately, he paused, then allowed himself to smile as his eyes carefully followed the shape of a narrow pipe running up to a water drain at the base of the northeast redoubt.

Quickly, he removed his rucksack, rummaged through the contents until he felt a nylon pouch. Removing the pouch, he unfolded the container, revealing a crossbow broken down into three parts. With lightning speed he attached the prod to the forestock and connected the string. Taking one of the razor-tipped quarrels, he pulled the string back, locking the string in the lock cover, then inserted the deadly bolt into the track.

The killing machine was ready. So was the killer.

Without hesitating, Phillips slipped quietly to the pipe where he took a grip and, without testing for stability, began pulling himself upward, hand over hand, moving up the wall like a spider.

In the redoubt, Awad dozed on the floor behind the sandbagged gun emplacement. The boy was tired, his nerves and strength raw from the lack of sleep. At his side, a small transistor played softly, the music soothing his fatigue.

Soon, he thought to himself, *it will be over. Now stand up. You must not let Jemal find you sleeping.* He pulled himself to his feet and staggered sleepily to the Ultimax, where he peered out over the shimmering water stretching north from the cove.

A sudden chill shook him, and turning, he thought for a moment that his fatigue had rid him of his senses. Peering over the edge of the sandbags, he stiffened as he saw a shadow lean out from the drainpipe.

A cruel face stared at him from behind a mask of camouflage paint!

Awad's eyes widened; his mouth started to open. His lips barely parted when Phillips fired the crossbow at point-blank range.

The razor-tipped quarrel hit Awad in the mouth with the force of a freight train. A long, cylindrical groove was carved through the boy's head, which exploded in the back as the quarrel erupted at the base of his skull, severing the pons of the medulla oblongata.

The force of the impact shot his feet straight out while his body pitched backward, flipping the Ashbal onto his back.

With feline grace, Phillips climbed into the redoubt where he checked the pulse at Awad's throat. Satisfied that the terrorist was dead, he took a heavy nylon rope from his rucksack, tied the rope off to a corner column, then fed the rope over the side.

Slattery was the first to appear, then Gunny. In less than sixty seconds the redoubt overflowed with the Red Cell team.

"Let's get to it," said Slattery, checking his watch.

"I hope the jet jocks aren't late," Gunny said, loading an M-79 grenade launcher.

"They won't be late." Slattery eased open the door of the redoubt. He could see the three remaining redoubts clearly. Across the way, he made out the shadowy image of a guard standing at a door.

"That's where they're holding the hostages," Slattery whispered to the others.

Closing the door carefully, he looked at the other SEALs. "When the shit hits the fan, you know what to do. Any questions?"

There were none.

Slattery took a starlight mask from his rucksack. "Put your masks on."

The SEALs put on the masks, which would protect them from the blinding light of the stun grenades, while letting them see in the dark.

Slattery checked his watch.

0329.

He leaned over the Ultimax, raising the flare gun that he gripped in one hand. Staring at his watch, he counted the seconds down. Thirty . . . Twenty . . . Ten . . . Five . . .

"It's time to rock and roll."

Slattery squeezed the trigger. A long, white tongue of iridescent fire spit from the muzzle, streaking upward in a majestic arc. When it reached the zenith, the canister exploded, releasing a golden flare that filled the sky with a brilliant dancing cloud of white.

54

"FANGS OUT!" SACRETTE SHOUTED INTO THE microphone.

Followed by a wave of seven F-18 Strikers, the *Crunch 'n' Munch* streaked toward the Libyan coastline.

Shoving the throttle to full military power, Sacrette aimed his F-18 Hornet at the first Libyan tank he sighted. The tank sat at the east wall, near the cove.

"This is for Munchy," he said, releasing a 500-pound laser-guided bomb from his right wing.

The bomb traveled in a clean flight path toward the Libyan tank.

Moments later, a thunderous explosion rocked the ground outside the villa.

The blackness was erased by a sudden flash of white-hot light; then a fiery red enveloped the grounds, rising in a long flat cloud. The air shook as the concussion ricocheted off the walls and spread back toward the other tanks, ripping many Libyan soldiers from their sleep, while sending others to an infinitive sleep.

Sacrette banked his Hornet as Blade made his run. Another explosion followed as the deadly bomb found its target, dissolving a Libyan tank at the west wall.

* * *

"Now!" Slattery shouted.

The door of the redoubt opened. Gunny leaned through, firing his M-79 at the northeast redoubt. The popping of the grenade was followed by a loud explosion as the grenade struck the door at the precise moment when it was opened by the young Ashbal Rashid.

Rashid didn't feel anything. The projectile struck him in the chest, exploding on impact with such suddenness there was no time to experience fear. Or pain.

Doc fired a LAWs rocket at the southwest redoubt adjacent to their position. A long tongue of fire seemed to join the two positions momentarily.

Inside the redoubt, Ziad was lifted from his feet by the explosion, which suddenly appeared as a wall of red. Flung backward, he pitched over the sandbags, falling toward the ground.

He tried to scream, to enjoy that one final gift a dying martyr should enjoy, but nothing came out.

Before he hit the ground he looked down in freefall. The pale light from the surrounding explosions shone on his chest. He felt himself shiver, then grew sick.

His chest was gone, replaced by a gaping hole that spewed red with his blood.

Ziad hit the ground in a dull-sounding heap.

Gunny had reloaded and fired at the last redoubt on the northwest corner. The grenade clapped in a loud thunderous explosion, ripping the walls apart.

A shrill scream was heard as Hassan's flesh was stripped from his body by the ravaging torrent of flying shards enveloping the redoubt.

"Four terrs down," Slattery called into the microphone hooked to his assault harness.

In the CIC, Captain Lord heard the steely voice of

the SEAL commander break the agonizing silence of the command center.

He said nothing. He continued to pace in a tight circle.

At the initial explosion. Ilyannha Lavi jerked from the floor and ran for the board where her splinter waited, the only weapon.

"Get up!" she shouted on the dead run. "They are here!"

The children lurched into their groups. Raanan went to the door where he crouched off to one side.

When the door opened, Layla and Mohammad charged through, their AK-47's blazing a sea of twisting, cutting steel into the darkness.

Raanan came up fast, extending his long leg in a vicious roundhouse kick. His foot struck the point of Mohammad's mandible, snapping the jaws and driving the splintered hinges into his brain. The Ashbal crumpled in a death throe.

Raanan kicked again, at the second terrorist.

With her night vision impaired by the burst of outside light, Layla saw nothing. She felt the kick, spun sideways, then crashed into the corner where a group of children crouched, away from her field of fire.

With the suddenness of a striking snake, the children began punching and kicking their captor, striking at the figure who tried to escape their clutches. The wrath of their torment spilled from their young arms and feet as kicks, harsh and damaging, found their mark in Layla's face and stomach.

"Kill her!" one shouted.

"Tear out her eyes!" shouted another.

Standing at the board, Ilyannha saw the girl's AK-47 lying on the floor in a rectangle of light.

She darted for the weapon.

Suddenly a tall, wiry figure appeared in the doorway.

"Kill them all. Kill the hostages," came the shout of Jemal, from somewhere outside.

Kahlil stood in the doorway. His weapon started to come up. He couldn't see, but he felt movement.

He swerved to the corner. His finger started to close around the trigger when he felt a rush of air coming toward him from the darkness near the window.

He turned to the advance, squeezed his trigger, and in the muzzle flash saw that his bullets had missed the Israeli girl, Ilyannha.

Ilyannha didn't miss. Her arm came down in a violent arc.

"Aaa-ggg-hhh!" Kahlil screamed. His eye burned as though touched with fire. He dropped his weapon, staggering backward while holding his face.

Reaching the light of the doorway he saw blood filling his hand. He reached to touch his eye. He felt pain again as his fingers touched the wooden splinter sunk deep into the optic nerve.

"Turn around," said a voice as cold as death.

Kahlil straightened. He was staring with his good eye at the helicopter parked below. Rage filled him as he realized he was being betrayed.

"Jemal!"

Jemal was climbing into the helicopter. On the co-pilot's side, Mustapha opened the door hurriedly and climbed inside, dragging his AK-47.

Kahlil started walking along the terrace.

"Stop," ordered Ilyannha, aiming the AK-47 at her former captor.

Kahlil stumbled forward, ignoring her while he concentrated on his newfound source of hatred.

As he reached the steps leading down to the courtyard, Ilyannha fired the weapon.

Kahlil shook violently as a storm of deadly bullets tore through his back. Rising on his toes, he seemed to glide forward, then pitched into the air above the steps and disappeared.

Ilyannha walked forward, her weapon at the ready. A sudden sound at her rear made her stop. She whirled, ready to fire.

"No!" shouted a voice. "We're Americans. Put down the weapon!"

Major Deke Slattery was walking toward her, his Uzi trained on the girl he had seen kill the terrorist. A slight smile cracked his lips as he approached her cautiously.

"Are you alright?" he asked softly.

She nodded. The weapon slipped from her hands, clattering off the tile flooring of the terrace.

Before she could answer, the thunderous roar of the helicopter split the muggy air.

"Get down!" Slattery pushed her down.

The JetRanger helicopter rose in a cloud of swirling, stirring dust and smoke.

Slattery stood, bringing his Uzi to bear on the copilot's side of the helicopter.

The face of a young boy appeared, frightened and confused. Suddenly the barrel of his weapon was coming through the opened door.

"Don't do it. Damn you!" Slattery said hatefully. "Don't make me kill you!"

Mustapha raised his weapon, aiming the barrel at Slattery.

In the last instant, Slattery squeezed the trigger. Holes filled the canopy; there were spiderweb streaks where the bullets ruptured the Plexiglas window of the door.

Mustapha pitched over violently; the helicopter yawwed crazily, then settled as Jemal pushed the dead Ashbal's body through the door.

The boy fell fifteen feet, and lay dead in the courtyard, sprawled like a broken doll beneath his fleeing leader.

The JetRanger banked, then disappeared over the west wall of the Villa de Valentino where the explosions of the bombed tanks continued among a din of screams.

Slattery took the microphone. Leaning over the rail, he stared down at the dead Palestinian terrorist. "Home Plate, this is Red Cell leader. The villa is ours. Launch the evacuation force." He paused, turning to Ilyannha. "Who was in the helicopter?"

"Mohammad Abu Jemal. The leader."

Slattery reported back to the CIC. "Repeat. The villa is ours. One escaped in a helicopter. Tell Thunderbolt it's his buddy from the *World Friendship*."

"Good job, Red Cell leader. Will pass the message on. Have helo on radar. The marines will arrive in five minutes with the evacuation force. Have your people ready."

"Roger," Slattery concluded the report, then turned to see Gunny approaching.

"What do we do with this one?" the tough marine asked. He was pulling a wide-eyed boy by the collar of his fatigue shirt.

Looking at Ilyannha, Slattery asked, "What's his name?"

She stared coldly at the boy. "Meheisi."

Slattery looked at Gunny. "Paddle the little snake's young ass, then cuff him. He'll go back with us."

Slattery followed Ilyannha into the hostage room. The children stood around in a large circle. Breaking through the circle, Slattery looked at their prize.

Layla lay motionless on her side.

"Jesus," Slattery whispered. A sickening wave of nausea swept over him as he stared at the dead Palestinian girl.

She no longer had a face.

Ilyannha touched Slattery on the shoulder. "Are you going to take us out of here?"

Before he could answer, a distant rumble could be heard from outside. Looking up, Slattery recognized the throaty growl of approaching aircraft.

Speaking into the microphone, he told the CIC, "We've got company."

55

0400.

THE AERIAL KNIFE FIGHT BEGAN WITH A CALM ORDER from the Fighting Hornets' squadron commander.

"Go to combat spread! I'll approach from Angel's fifteen. Four-thousand-foot step-up. We'll take them from out of the rising sun," Sacrette ordered the fighters of VFA-101 as seven MiG-25 Foxbats appeared on his radar scope.

Sacrette's F-18, and four fighters from the TAC CAP screamed east to engage the approaching Libyan fighters. Domino and two F-18s remained as Tactical Air Cover for attacking aircraft, to protect the evacuation, while the seven strikers continued to pummel the terrain outside the villa and to protect the highway approach from Tobruk.

Spread in a wide formation that looked like geese returning to Canada, the F-18s were separated by 4000-foot intervals.

Streaking from eight miles west at 35,000 feet above the Libyan desert, the MiGs were BVR, beyond visual range, and, with the darkness, would remain unseen until they were nose to nose with the Hornets.

Sacrette flipped the weapons select switch on the HOTAS to "missiles," readying the deadly Sidewinder and Sparrow missiles on his wingtip and wingpods.

"Fangs out!" came the excited cry from Blade, who was aft of Sacrette at his five o'clock position.

Sacrette narrowed his eyes, and just above the gunsight he saw a dark spot suddenly spread into seven smaller dots as the MiGs approached at supersonic speed.

"Good," Sacrette said over the microphone. "They're at supersonic." He eased back on the throttle, telling the Fighting Hornets, "Let's slow the game down."

While most aerial engagements are fought with missiles at great distances, the F-18 is the best close-in fighter in the world. Dogfighting is an art of gaining position superiority, not a game of speed. Turns and maneuvering are the key to getting the opponent in a shooting position.

While the F-18 is not the fastest aircraft in the world, it's the best turning aircraft in the sky. It's the turn radius that allows the pilot to shake, or dog an opponent in ACM, air combat maneuvering.

The F-18s jumped onto the MiGs from below.

"Let's cut down the odds. Give them a Fox two spread," Sacrette ordered.

"Lock-on, and Fox two," shouted Blade, as a heat-seeking missile streaked from beneath his wing.

"Fox two," called Axeman.

"Fox two," piped up Lt. Steven Keiling, call sign "Killer."

"Fox two," Sacrette said calmly.

Four long, red fiery tails etched the black sky. On Sacrette's radar screen, he could see the MiGs breaking formation as the Libyan pilots went to evasive.

Seconds later, a red fireball lit the graying morning with a mushrooming cloud of death.

"Yeah!" shouted Blade, getting his first kill.

The fireball no more than appeared when another ruptured on the horizon. "Two down," shouted Killer.

Sacrette's missile struck the lead MiG, who was coming out of an avalanche evasive move.

"Three down."

"Mine missed," came the disappointed voice of Axeman.

Glancing at the radar scope, Sacrette could see the Foxbats were taking up attack positions.

"We're one-on-one!" Sacrette shouted. "Take what you can get."

Too close for missiles, the F-18 pilot selected a target and went after the MiGs.

Sacrette took a MiG at his ten o'clock high. He switched the weapons selector to guns, so that the deadly M61-A1 20mm cannon could compute enemy airspeed, attitude, g factor, and bullet time to reach the target.

Unless the MiG changed direction as Sacrette fired, the bullets would score.

"God dammit!" Sacrette swore. "Missed!"

The MiG must have read his mind.

It was one-on-one. The deadliest, fastest game in the sky.

Blade and a Lib shot at each other nose to nose. As the Flogger screamed past the Lib pilot rolled, cranked off a one-eighty, rolling out beneath Blade's six.

A fiery streak shot from the MiG's undercarriage.

"I'm locked up!" screamed Blade, whose canopy was filling with the screeching siren of eminent death as a MiG AA-8 Aphid missile locked on to his Hornet's heat signature.

Blade Zone Fived the Hornet, streaking for the deck, the missile in trail. Unable to outrun the Mach 3.0

capability of the Aphid, Blade did what only the Hornet could do at that speed.

He hammered a 7-g bat-turn, pulling the Hornet back on line with the MiG. A racking tongue of machine-gun fire spewed from the Flogger, narrowly missing Blade.

"Eat this, mother!" Blade shouted as the Flogger passed off his wingtip.

The Aphid, having picked up on the MiG's heat source, tracked onto the Libyan aircraft.

A fireball of death filled the sky as the MiG ate its own missile.

"Yeah!" shouted Blade. "Yeah!"

Sacrette was busy with a Flogger on his tail. The MiG was on guns, the way Sacrette liked to play the game.

"Come on, baby," he called to the MiG. "Let's see your stuff."

In air combat, the "scissors" maneuver seems to have been invented for the Hornet.

Sacrette went to afterburner vertical, leading the MiG to 35,000 feet in a 7.4 g pure vertical climb. Reaching the top, Sacrette's aileron rolled into a nose-down position, diving straight for the earth.

Falling over the top, the MiG was on Sacrette's tailpipes. Before Sacrette reached ninety degrees attitude, he neutralized the MiG with a hard right turn, swinging outward, extending his flight path into a loop, while slowing his airspeed.

The MiG, unable to maneuver as quickly, remained at the ninety-degree attitude.

The Foxbat shot past Sacrette, who looked up and could see the AA-6 and AA-8 missiles on the MiG's underbelly.

Quickly Sacrette brought his nose up in a g-turn that pushed him deep into his seat.

Right or left? Sacrette asked himself, trying to figure the MiG's next directional move to shake the Hornet.

It was a game of the best hunch for this split second.

Sighting the MiG to his front, Sacrette rolled left, anticipating the MiG would go evasive to the right.

The hunch rang down the curtain on the Lib's final act.

"Gotcha!" Sacrette said throatily as the tunnel vision from the maneuver began to clear, giving him the most beautiful unprotected ass of an airplane he'd ever seen.

"Pure pussy!" Sacrette said with an evil grin.

The MiG's tail was as clear as the sun now, sitting flush on the horizon from 25,000 feet.

"I got your ass now, sweet cookie!" Sacrette squeezed the trigger on the 20mm cannon.

The guns flashed a river of bullets that seemed to join the two aircraft for a single deadly moment.

Suddenly smoke exploded from the MiG's tail.

In the next instant Sacrette could see the Foxbat's canopy jettison system launch the pilot in a long rocketing trajectory.

It was over as fast as it began.

"Five down!" Sacrette called excitedly.

"And two heading for the barn," Axeman piped up in a voice of sheer exuberance.

Looking to the west, Sacrette made out the images of the two remaining MiGs, beating a path back to their base in Tobruk.

Pressing the microphone, Sacrette issued an order to the F-18 fighter pilots of VFA-101. "Return to TAC CAP. I'll rejoin you on the carrier."

"Where are you going?" asked Blade.

Sacrette looked at his radar screen. A single blip was burning along the coastline sector.

"I've got to talk to a man about the proper way to treat a lady," was Sacrette's only reply.

Hitting Zone Five, the Hornet darted west on a tongue of fire for the last play in the game.

56

SACRETTE HAD MONITORED THE TRANSMISSION FROM Slattery to Home Plate and, seeing the JetRanger depart the villa, had remained with the fighters.

After the knife fight with the Libyans, it took Sacrette less than five minutes to jump onto the helicopter's tail. The JetRanger was flying low along the coastline, hugging the natural outcroppings of cliffs and ridges for protection.

The sun was beginning to purple the sky as the first traces of light crawled over the eastern horizon, thinning the blanket of darkness shrouding the desert.

With each passing second the helicopter grew more clear.

Clarity was what Sacrette wanted. He needed to be certain there was no doubt in Jemal's mind.

"Let's go eyeball to eyeball, Jemal."

Sacrette closed in on the helicopter from the rear, easing back on the power while lowering flaps and landing gear.

Moving onto the JetRanger's port, the fighter pilot glanced over at Jemal, who was staring wild-eyed, with that special fear that always marks the face of the pursued.

The Hornet and JetRanger were less than ten feet apart, flying side by side.

Reaching into his flight suit, Sacrette retrieved a small object he had brought with him from the *Valiant*, should just such a moment arise.

Jemal looked at the cockpit of the Hornet. It took several seconds for him to recognize what the pilot was holding. When he did, his face went slack.

"Remember me?" Sacrette asked the terrorist, waving a miniature flag at Jemal.

The red maple leaf of the Canadian flag that Sacrette held left Jemal with no doubt as to his pursuer's identity.

Fear took hold of Jemal. Realizing he was doomed in an aerial mismatch, he shoved the nose of the helicopter forward, diving for the sanctuary of the cliffs fringing the coastline.

Flying "down and dirty," the F-18 Hornet screamed by as the helicopter auto-rotated in a tight spiral beneath the fighter.

"God dammit!" Sacrette cursed. Anticipating Jemal's intentions, he cleaned up the flaps and gear, went to full military power, then turned back to where the helicopter was darting in and out of the cliffs.

In the JetRanger, Jemal recovered from the spiral as a long stretch of beach appeared. Without hesitating, he cut the power and crunched the helicopter to a sudden landing in the shadows of a towering wall of rock.

Sacrette set up for a gun-run but saw it was too late.

The elusive Jemal had jumped from the helicopter and was sprinting toward the cliff. Reaching the protection of the cliff, the terrorist disappeared into a cave carved into the cliff by centuries of pounding surf.

Sacrette gave the situation momentary thought

while he examined the terrain and the mile-long stretch of beach. Finally, he made a decision.

"You tricky bastard," Sacrette said somewhat admiringly. "Two can play at this game."

His decision wasn't based on sound judgment, nor good military sense. He could rocket and bomb the cliff, but would never know with certainty if the terrorist had been killed.

After all, he reminded himself, Jemal had made the world think he was dead when the *World Friendship* exploded.

Therefore, he tried to convince himself, the decision was one based on need. The duel had become more than personal. The need to see the man lying dead at his feet as retribution was one thing; the innocent people who might suffer in the future was another.

It had become imperative that Mohammad Abu Jemal's treachery no longer threatened the world.

But first things first!

The quarry was on the ground with a helicopter.

Sacrette took aim on the outline of the helicopter, then squeezed the firing mechanism.

A long tongue of rattling machine-gun fire breathed from the nose, joining the JetRanger and Hornet with a momentary stream of lightning-white heat.

Instantly the JetRanger dissolved in a thunderous roar, spewing metal and fire in a mushrooming cloud of destruction.

Inside the cave, Jemal felt the walls shake; cones of stalactites fell around him like heavenly spears.

The long throaty groan of the F-18 Hornet punctuated the sky along the beach as Sacrette's Strike/Fighter shot like an arrow toward a point east of the cave.

His hand squeezed the bomb release. A single MK

84 2000-pound bomb arced for the rocky wall. The impact sent a geyser of rock spewing outward from the wall.

Smoke and flying rock filled the air. A landslide flowed with massive boulders crashing into the sea, reshaping the wall into a rocky barrier stretching out into the Mediterranean.

"Allah!" Jemal screamed. "What is that dog trying to do?" Stumbling forward, he ran to the mouth of the cave.

A quick glance down the east end of the beach gave him a chilling answer.

The F-18 was approaching low on the horizon.

Sacrette could see where the receding surf darkened the beach into a compacted surface that was as hard as concrete.

Turning on final approach, he raised the nose three degrees and eased back on the throttle, beginning a high sinking landing.

Easing the right wing down five degrees, he countermeasured with five degrees left sideslip, holding the aircraft steady while continuing to raise the nose to five degrees, then seven degrees until the Hornet began to settle.

"This is not a carrier landing," Sacrette said out loud, reminding himself of the different landings. "Land-based landing. Short field over an obstacle. Grease it on, nice and smooth."

When the rear gear greased onto the beach, he held backpressure on the HOTAS, keeping the nose gear off the ground until the Hornet had bled off sufficient speed for landing.

Feeling the nose dive forward as the nose gear settled onto the beach, Sacrette eased the power to neutral.

Raising the cockpit, he climbed down from the Hornet and ran across the sand, leaving the Strike/Fighter running in low idle.

At the mouth of the cave he knelt and examined the entrance.

One set of footprints could be seen. The sand kicked out at the rear of the imprints, indicating that the tracks were made by someone going into the cave.

Jemal was trapped in the cave.

Sacrette slipped inside the cave, pausing behind a large boulder to catch his breath.

The cave was dark and muggy; the air stifling and hot.

"Hello, American." The voice of Jemal came from the rear of the cave.

"What can I do for you, hotshot?" Sacrette replied. He was inching over the rock, trying to pinpoint the origin of the voice.

A burst of automatic weapon fire snaked along the rock, twisting and kicking the sand in a steely march to the left of Sacrette.

Noting that the bullets moved at a right angle away from him, he judged Jemal was on the left side of the cave.

"Close. But not close enough, asshole!" Sacrette shouted. "You don't get a merit badge for marksmanship. What's the matter? Can't you hit anything unless it's closer than two feet?"

Another burst of fire swept the entrance, pushing Sacrette into a huddled position as the bullets danced at a left angle, chewing away at the rock.

"That's better. But still no Kewpie doll."

He's moved to the opposite side of the cave, thought Sacrette.

"Tell me, American. Why do you wish to die so far from home?" Jemal taunted.

"That's a good question. One you might consider."

"You Americans are very foolish. You think you can go anywhere and do anything. My friends will come soon. All I have to do is wait. Be patient."

Sacrette smirked at the impudence. "What friends? They're all dead. All those treacherous little bastards!"

Jemal screamed in rage, "You fucker! I will cut your heart out!" A blinding wall of bullets stormed from Jemal's position.

"Not in this life, slick. You had your chance on the water. When I was helpless. Now it's just you and me. *Mano y mano*. What do you say, Jemal. Just an old-fashioned hangtown shootout. You and me. One-on-one? You've got the balls to kill defenseless women and children. How are you against a man?"

Sacrette waited. He needed some reply to make his move. He heard nothing. Cautiously, he leaned over the rock and fired his pistol five times. The bullets thudded against the rear wall. Several ricocheted off the rocks, filling the musky air with a distinctive whine.

"Check mate," Sacrette whispered to himself.

Carefully, he withdrew from the rocks, racing toward the F-18 Hornet parked on the hardened sand.

The hunt was on . . . this time, on his terms!

57

JEMAL SAT AT THE BACK OF THE CAVE. GONE WERE his thoughts of a Palestinian state. Gone were his dreams of returning his people to their homeland. Gone was his notion of martyrdom.

Survival was on his mind.

The entrance of the cave loomed before him like a giant passageway to freedom. Or to paradise.

He had not heard the American in several minutes. The silence was gnawing at his nerves.

"American," he called. "You have come a long way from your home to die."

There was no reply.

Again he shouted. "American. Why does your government want to kill Palestinians?"

Again there was no reply.

There was only the sound of a high-pitched whir.

The blood in Jemal's veins turned to jelly as he recognized the familiar sound of a winding turbine approaching the cave.

Sacrette sat in the cockpit of the *Crunch 'n' Munch*, easing forward the power of the port engine, allowing the Strike/Fighter to turn toward the opening of the cave.

As the nose turned to a forty-five-degree angle into

the mouth of the cave, Sacrette paused, then shouted over the roar of the engines. "Here's my answer, you son of a bitch!"

His finger closed around the trigger harnessing the M61-A1 Gatling gun positioned just forward of the cockpit.

The earth shook as the massive 20mm rounds fired point-blank into the cave opening, sweeping the entrance as Sacrette worked the aircraft slowly around until the nose nearly looked squarely into the place where Jemal was hiding.

The hurricane force of bullets took Jemal in a giant wave of steel, lifting his body into the air where the impact carried him against the rear wall.

His only thoughts were of the stinging, biting misery tearing him as he hung there for several long seconds while the bullets and flying rock continued to tear at his body.

His legs were chewed off at the knees; his shoulders separated at the chest. His face turned to ooze as the hammering tore his eyes from his skull, then erased all evidence of his existence.

Finally, the torrent subsided, replaced by the acrid odor of gunpowder and death fuming the cave with its special smell and taste.

Thirty seconds after he began firing in the 6000-round-per-minute mode, Sacrette released the trigger.

The M61-A1 fell quiet. Smoke wisped from the gun ports; other than the gradual ebb and flow of the surf, silence covered the beach.

The silence of death, and its aftermath; the knowledge that finally it was over.

Sacrette walked slowly into the cave. He was certain

Jemal was dead. Yet, for his own personal satisfaction, he had to look on the man's dead face.

He was a fighter pilot. He was a killer from the heavens, not from the ground. He did so with calm deadly precision and cunning.

Perhaps it was time to answer the question that had plagued him since he realized his first kill.

What did it look like?

Walking to the rear of the cave, he flashed the light from a survival flashlight off the floor and walls. The interior was devastated. Deep holes carved tracks along the floor, roof, walls, everywhere.

He found Jemal lying covered in sandy rubble. There was nothing left to identify the man as human.

Slowly, Sacrette turned and started away.

Five minutes later the roar of the F-18 Hornet punctured the air above the cave as Sacrette lifted off, raised the nose to seventy-five degrees, and shot straight up on a pure afterburner climb.

At Angel's twenty-three he leveled off, then Zone Fived the afterburner again, leaving a Mach-1 sonic boom in his trail as a reminder of his presence to the Libyans, and any other entity who might be looking for trouble with the innocent.

Should they try again, Commander Boulton Sacrette, and others like him, would be waiting.

They would be waiting!

Epilogue

THE NUCLEAR CARRIER USS *VALIANT* HAD NEVER AP-peared more beautiful, nor more victorious to Com-mander Boulton Sacrette.

His fuel was nearly bingo, but he didn't mind, he could land on the fumes, or carry the Strike/Fighter across the deck on his own will and exuberance.

"Call the ball, Thunderbolt. You're cleared for land-ing," came the voice of the Air Ops officer.

Lining up the fresnel lens, a bright yellow light that acts as a glideslope indicator, Thunderbolt Sacrette re-plied, "Roger. Thunderbolt zero-point-two." This was his casual indication that he had 200 pounds of fuel re-maining.

There was no fuel left for a flyby. There was only wire three.

Sacrette came over the threshold in a whisper, crunched the trap, grappling wire three as he shoved the power to full military.

The wire held the Hornet to the deck.

A human wave swelled forward, cheering, clapping: thousands of fighting men of the USS *Valiant*.

And twenty-four grateful children from the *World Friendship*.

Ilyannha Lavi ran with the others to the wing of the *Crunch 'n' Munch*, watching with anticipation as the tall figure stood at the cockpit amid a sea of cheering sailors and marines.

He has good eyes, she thought, as he removed his helmet and bowed arrogantly at the swarm.

For five days she and the others had held on to the prayer that someone like him would come to their rescue.

Here he was. A hero.

Fresh from the fight.

As he stepped down from the ladder, she threw her arms around his neck. "Shalom, Boulton Sacrette. Thank you from all of us."

The children stood beaming at the CAG. Behind the children stood the Fighting Hornets of VFA-101.

They appeared tired. Worn. Ready for the next fight.

"Cold. Bold. And bad to the bone!" they shouted in harmony.

Slattery stepped forward, his hand extended.

They shook hands for a long moment. Gone was the muzzle flash smile of the SEAL commander. He stared admiringly at the man who had stood at his side during the fight.

"Semper Fi, Thunderbolt," Slattery said firmly.

"Fangs out!" replied Sacrette, echoing the battle cry of the fighter pilot.

Tilting his head sideways, Slattery thought he noticed something strange in Sacrette's face. "You've seen the Dragon."

Remembering the riddled body of Jemal, Sacrette replied, "I've seen the Dragon up close."

Slattery understood. He had tasted and seen the fiery breath of the Death Dragon dozens of times. Each time it changed him, made him harder. Tougher. More determined to survive.

Diamonds Farnsworth fought his way through the crowd and embraced Sacrette. He went apoplectic when he saw that the undercarriage of the Hornet was chewed up from the beach takeoff.

"What in the name of everything precious did you do to my aircraft? Sir!" Farnsworth demanded.

Sacrette put his arm around Farnsworth. The chief's bulldog face turned into a shining grin.

"What I always do, Chief. I took her to the edge of the envelope . . . and brought her home. That's my job. Getting her fresh for the next ball is your job."

Farnsworth clapped Sacrette on the back. "She'll be ready."

At that moment the crowd seemed to part as Captain Elrod Lord strode forward, his square-rigged shoulders set as though they were made of oak.

Sacrette saluted. "Captain."

Lord extended his hand. "The Secretary General of the United Nations has asked me to convey a message to you, Commander Sacrette, and to you, Major Slattery."

They waited for the words that would end the operation, and key them for the next mission.

"Well done."

The most precious words in naval language.

The flight deck exploded with applause.

Taking Sacrette by the elbow, Lord steered the commander of the air group toward the island, threading through the path that opened for them in the human wall.

The SEALs followed, as did Ilyannha and the children.

Farnsworth hurried to Sacrette's side, where he saw Captain Lord lean and shout over the din into the CAG's ear.

"We've been reassigned."

"Where are we going?"

"Stateside for two months to outfit, then we're deploying to the Caribbean."

Sacrette pulled to a stop, halting the human parade that followed in his trail.

"What's our mission?"

Lord laughed. "It seems the president has some notions about using American military force to interdict drug trafficking moving out of Central America."

Farnsworth didn't hear Sacrette's reply.

He didn't have to. He saw his eyes.

They were shining.

Another hunt was on!

Tom Willard lives in Grand Forks, North Dakota. He is a Vietnam veteran.